The Slave Traders of Umbinga

By Cheryl Castro

Isa 40:31

Eagle's Wings Publishing
ewpublishing.com

Published by
Eagle's Wings Publishing
Medford, OR 97501

2013 ©Cheryl Castro

Cover Illustration By Emily Burdge

ISBN-10: 0-615-79810-1
ISBN-13: 978-0-615-79810-3

The Slave Traders of Umbinga

By Cheryl Castro

Table of Contents

Prologue 1
Things to come 3
Discoveries 8
Celebration 13
The Gatherer 18
Safe Keeping 22
Alone 28
Preparations 32
Disaster 38
Aleeta Gets Company 43
Help From Across the Sea 48
On the Edge 56
Tracking 60
Arrival 66
Placement 71
Dree 76
A Sacrifice 81
Among the Umbingas 87
The Road Ahead 93
The Royal Residence 98
The Gathering 103
Journey's End 109
Inside 115
Spies into the City 120
Deadly Confrontation 125
Together Again 131
Finding Luwanna 137
Rescue 142
The Moving Rocks 151
Celebrating Home 156
The Future 161
Epilogue 166

Prologue

Uri, now seventeen, faces an uncertain future.

Graduated from school, he must decide where to live. Should he stay with his sister Beka and her husband Suwat, or with his true family, across the sea in Dombara Land?

Seventeen years ago, kidnapped and brought to the Pinola village as a baby, he became part of a wonderful family. Then at fourteen he was taken against his will to Dombara Land where he met his real parents. In this strange land, Uri struggled to find his way back across the Green Sea, to the Pinola village. Along the way, Uri acquired a new faith in the Creator of All. His Pinola family and the whole tribe believed in evil spirits that roamed the land. Bringing the new faith back to the Pinolas, he came up against those who chose to be adversaries of The Way.

He experienced many traumas while seeking the Pinola men who had decided to bring evil upon the new believers and he found himself following them to back to Dombara Land. One good thing... it led to a bonding with his Dombara people. However it left him feeling awkward and wondering what to do with the rest of his life. He spent the last few years attending school in Pinola land, and spent summer break with the Dombara people.

Rill, whom Uri believe died in a raging storm on the Green Sea, had survived and now had nothing but evil and revenge in his heart for Uri. This year, as Uri visited his family and friends in Dombara Land, a new and frightening event took place while he attended a joyous celebration. Will he lose his beloved Luwanna to his demented adversary, Rill? Uri must rely on faith, and knowledge that The Creator will not desert him. This belief is the only thing he has to lean on while struggling against the overwhelming odds.

In order to rescue the captured women, Uri and his friends travel through a strange, cold land below the Bast village. Far south and more dangerous than anywhere he has gone in the past. Not only does he come up against Rill, but also discovers a people with a strange, cruel, and foreign way of life.

He finds himself in a struggle with the concept of his Lord's omniscient power, and the old, old question. Why do bad things happen to the innocent and pure?

Chapter One

Things to come

A thick mist rose up from the wet and soggy ground. The mist appeared to emanate from the silence that surrounded Uri, and felt wet and heavy on his bare arms. Where was he and why? Nevertheless, Uri perceived he was looking for someone. The unfamiliar surroundings produced a clouded and troubled perception of the details around him.

Out of nowhere, a face emerged. A slit appeared, and a tongue poked out.

"Hey, lookin' for someone?" The slit across the face behaved like a mouth, opening wide. A gravelly voice taunted, "Haa, haa."

The voice seemed familiar, and it produced a foreboding chill that traveled over Uri's body. He struggled to speak, but nothing came out. The mist parted enough for Uri to make out the figure in front of him. It was a grotesque caricature of Rill. He squatted on the road, grey, round and bloated.

Uri recoiled. His stomach turned over. This image reminded him of a bug that inhabited the Pinola desert, a pron. When touched, a smelly greenish liquid leaked out. Uri wanted to squash Rill, as he would the pron, but no matter how he tried, he was not able to move.

This Rill-like creature laughed as he hopped back and forth, "Ha, ha, ha. I have her, and my friend, you will never see her again." It spoke with a croaking, tormenting sound, and beckoned Uri to come forward.

No matter how hard Uri tried to lift his arms, they were much too heavy. He looked at his feet and saw they had grown roots that penetrated deep into the ground. Uri twisted in anguish. He groaned, aching to move, aching to get his hands on Rill. He knew he could not stand much more. It was overwhelming, and the torture ate away at the very core of his being.

The next instant Uri opened his eyes, and gazed bewildered into the darkness of his bedroom. He sat up in bed. Sweat rolled down his face and neck. He ached from head to toe.

What had just happened? It seemed so real, so frightening. However, Uri was still in Pinola Land, and the dream was quickly relegated to the misty area of dreamland.

Oh, Lord, my Creator, he thought, *was this only a dream or could it be...a vision?*

Uri got out of bed and went into the kitchen. He stood at the window looking into Beka's yard, bathed in moonlight, and dipped his hand in the water jar, wiping his face.

What would happen next? Was his dream a warning, or only fear playing with his mind? He had wanted a gift of prophecy and vision, when he first accepted the New Belief. *"Well, be careful what you ask for."* he thought. Now he might have to learn how to deal with this "blessing."

Uri knew many more problems would arise, and his life would change many times. He couldn't let this dream affect him. He must be ready and have a firm belief that The Creator would guide him through all the predicaments and troubles he would encounter in his life.

He looked outside at the peaceful moonlit scene once more, then made his way back to bed wondering if this might be the last time he would sleep in his bed in Beka's home. When he left for Dombara Land, he had no plans to return in the near future.

Not able to fall back to sleep, Uri lay quietly with his eyes closed, but at the first sign of dawn he left his bed and made his way to his favorite spot on the dunes. In two days he was to leave for Dombara Land, and Uri had promised to meet with his Yoka teacher, Ceshori today.

The sand dunes of the Pinola landscape heaved and dipped along the horizon, revealing an endless panorama of sand and sky. Uri sat cross-legged, looking up while feeling the Terrasian sunrise warm the morning air. His mind groped for answers to the most important questions of his life. What to do and where to live? He longed to stay with his Pinola sister, Beka, and the wonderful friends like Denar and Abosol. Torn, Uri still longed for Dombara Land, with Luwanna, Coran and his real family. It was there he could continue an education, and figure out what he needed to learn in order to find an occupation.

Close in front of him the sand shivered. A wona was working its way through the sand to find a lizard for breakfast. He casually watched as it moved away. There was no desire in him to be that "great hunter" he once believed was so important. Strange how that thought consumed him only a few years ago. Now seventeen years old, his life had taken a different turn.

As Uri's mind wandered, he noticed someone, a distance away, approaching him. During the course of the school year, Uri had related to Ceshori about the abandoned dwellings he and his friends came upon on their search for Zekod. Ceshori had been intrigued. He was obsessed with all things ancient and formed strange theories of how all the tribes dispersed into the various areas of the two continents. Now was the time to take Ceshori to the dwellings

Uri stood and waved. The teacher was small, his head shaved Yoka style. He wore a large ring through the top of his right ear. The color of his eyes matched Beka's, but the features of Yoka's were clearly different from the Pinola people. Yokas had broad noses and only a trace of eyebrows. Their faces were wide, and included high sharp cheekbones. All Yoka people wore tunics, and invented a type of shoe where a strap, threaded from the bottom of the sole, pulled up through the toes around the ankle. It was very sturdy, made from woven strands of the long, thin leaves of a desert tree.

Uri was aware the tribe was highly intelligent and possessed an intense curiosity. They revered their teachers and looked to them for leadership. At the school, there was a model of the night sky. A schedule of the rising of the sun and the moons throughout the year held a prominent place in the classroom and in the customs of the tribe itself. They scheduled their planting and harvesting cycles around the star's and the two moons locations during the year. The Yoka tribe believed these things were important to know about. Without realizing it, Uri had picked up the Yoka's curiosity.

"I am ready to go to see these abandoned structures you told me about," Ceshori said.

"Fine, shall we return to the village and pack up?" Uri answered. "The trip will take us several hours. We can camp overnight on the way back."

"I don't want to be in a rush." Ceshori said. "I want to spend as much time at the dwellings as I need. I will bring some tools with me."

6

"Tools?" Uri asked

"Tools to examine any relics we may find."

"Oh, relics." Uri repeated, but he wasn't sure what Ceshori meant.

Chapter Two
Discoveries

It was afternoon when they arrived at the ancient ruins. Uri was surprised to see how Ceshori grew increasingly excited. The little man looked carefully through the first few dwellings, and then they came across the one with the blackened wall.

"Finding this village has extreme importance!" He gleefully exclaimed.

"Why?" asked Uri. To him it seemed simple enough. Here was a place people had fire for warmth or cooking.

Ceshori opened his bag of tools and carefully scraped a piece of the blacked wall onto a paper. "What did they burn in order to create this black stain? Was there a reason they chose that particular place? There are many questions." He wrapped the piece of paper to protect the contents, and placed them into the bag.

Making their way upward, Uri followed Ceshori to the top. He showed Uri where the dwellings had been carved from the rock face of the cliffs. As Ceshori looked at the ground, he walked in an expanding circle. A smile came over his face and he pointed to an area of small mounds. A digging tool appeared from Ceshori's bag and he carefully removed the top surface of dirt.

"Can you see them?" He asked Uri, who stepped forward and peered at what he thought were rock fragments.

"What am I looking for?" Uri squinted at the ground.

"These are broken pieces of pottery." Ceshori pointed to the fragments. "Very old." He cleared another spot. "Look, this was a grinding rock. They must have grown crops."

"Oh," Uri nodded. "Since they left behind clues to their way of life can we find out why they disappeared?"

"Maybe." Ceshori replied. He gathered some of the pieces of broken pottery and followed the same routine with the bag of tools.

Uri pointed to the rock face that sat near the top of the cliffs. "What do you think about that? When we first saw it, we couldn't be sure if it was naturally shaped that way, or maybe sculptured."

Ceshori left the pottery shards and walked up to the rock. He examined it from every angle.

"I think..." he circled it again. " I see no evidence of chipping on the rock. I would venture to say the people found it much as it looks now. Weather has left its mark and worn it down, but not much. I think this is why they built their homes here. They probably believed it was a god or something similar so they settled near it. Maybe made sacrifices to it."

Uri was stunned. "Sacrifices... like what?"

"Oh, animals, or first fruits of their harvest. If we can find blood stains around it, then we will have a better knowledge of what their beliefs were."

Ceshori spied a large flat rock that had tumbled down the hill. He scampered down to it, scraping, and wiping it off. He closely examined the rock. "I can't find evidence that shows anything."

He climbed back up to where Uri stood. "That's too bad. However, now that I know where this is located, I will come back another time, and bring my team of teachers."

"What will you do with this stuff you are collecting?" Uri asked.

"Examine it, do some simple tests. We don't have any knowledge of these remains. We learn by using our imagination and evaluate different possibilities.

Ceshori poked and prodded for several more minutes. He entered every one of the dwellings, gathering bits, and pieces of this and that. Then they started back down to the river and the long trip home.

They did not walk in silence. Ceshori discussed at length the beliefs he conjured up in his mind, and what it all meant. "I believe a civilization occupied this area hundreds of years ago, maybe thousands. Something happened that caused them to leave. Maybe it was a weather change, maybe food grew scarce."

"Where did they go?" Uri asked.

"Ah… that remains a mystery. Did they get in boats and sail away, or travel to another part of this land? Maybe some left and some stayed, moving west or south. Until we find clues as to what happened, we won't know."

Uri listened and contributed some of his ideas. "It could be they all got sick and died, or they were attacked and killed."

"Well then, where are the skeletons? We found no bones."

It was interesting to theorize, but Uri thought, whatever the truth was concerning the civilization that lived in these ruins eons ago, could not possibly affect his life in any way. His main concern had to do with the immediate future.

It grew late so they stopped near an outcrop of rocks. Settling in between them, they felt safe and comfortable. Uri started a fire, a skill he had perfected, and they warmed themselves, while consuming a simple meal of biscuits, fruit, and dried meat.

"By the way," Ceshori asked as he scooted closer to the night's campfire. "What are you going to do now that you have finished school here?"

"I have given much thought to the future. First, I am going to spend some time in Dombara Land and go to their school for a while. They have history and mathematic classes I would like to take."

"In history you will do well, but mathematics...?" the teacher chuckled.

"It can't hurt, and maybe I will begin to understand some of the basic principles, if I hear it from someone else's point of view." Uri said defensively.

"True. Even I need a higher understanding in order to prove my theories. Maybe I'll come with you." They laughed, and then Ceshori grew somber. "I will miss you. I will miss your sharp, inquiring mind."

Uri patted Ceshori's knee. They reached the village in the late morning. Ceshori went his way and Uri went back to the hut he shared with Beka and Suwat knowing his old teacher would work on the mystery of the ruins for a long time.

Beka had recently returned from her booth at the marketplace, and Uri found her in the kitchen.

"What are you doing?" Uri asked as he walked in.

"Preparing dinner." She answered smiling.

"Isn't it a little early?" Uri looked around for a snack.

"I have to prepare it first. Then I can relax for a while before I begin to cook." She stopped and turned to look at Uri.

"Have you decided what you are going to do, now that school is over?"

"Coran is arriving in the morning and I am going back with him. I don't want to miss Aleeta and Coran's betrothal celebration." Uri replied as he chomped down on a blue colored fruit.

"I know it is the best decision for your future, but I will miss you, terribly." She came over and put her arms around him, holding him tight.

"It will be hard to leave you and Suwat." Uri swallowed hard, fighting the lump in his throat.

"Well," Beka said, "it's not like we will never see you again. It will be a temporary separation."

"Right." Uri replied softly

That night Uri snuggled down in the comfort of his bed and drifted into a sleep that was broken by many strange dreams. Dreams of rocks and idols, mixed up with Rill, Luwanna, and Aleeta. He woke in the morning with an uneasy feeling of anxiety that didn't leave even after he had set sail with Coran.

Chapter Three

Celebration

A soft evening breeze moved tenderly across the tips of the leaves on the trees that outlined the horizon where the two moons continued their slow progress in their nightly trek across the Dombara sky. The play field, lit by dozens of torches, jumped and danced with a festive glow. Flowers were everywhere. Brightly colored ribbons, held high with wooden poles, fluttered in the breeze. The cho field was in the center of the park, so special gatherings took place off to the edge where bushes and trees stood silently in the dark in dense groups.

Several tables overflowed with fresh fruits, bits of sweets on colored trays, and meat cooked to perfection. The women were thrilled to cook their favorite foods for everyone to smack their lips over at these special occasions. However, tonight no one was looking at the sky, landscape, food, or decorations. Tonight everyone's eyes were on Aleeta.

There was an actual glow surrounding her. The blue dress flowed around her slim frame, and the flowers, coated with bits of shining specks, twinkled in her hair as she moved through the crowd. Her hair was no longer tied on the side, as young maidens wore, but hung in loose pale, brown waves. Her dark eyes and the color of her hair were the only mark of her Pinola origin. In soul and spirit, Aleeta was a Dombara and tonight she was giving herself to a Dombara man. They would become betrothed to each other and pledge a beginning of their life together.

The marriage would take place in a matter of weeks, but until then they would stay next to each other in special huts. Spending all their waking hours together they continually attended lessons by the high priest, Elari. They would learn about the significance of marriage, and learn how to spend a lifetime of living in unison.

Uri stood at the front with Bibbi and Elajon. Close behind was his mother Marga holding Sarella who squirmed about, trying to see through all the people. Uri had not been around to witness his sister Tika's and Koori's marriage, or Lyshon and Goth's either. This was the first time he attended a betrothal, and he was enjoying every minute of it.

Captivated by Aleeta's beauty as she proceeded down the opening in the crowd, he could hardly remember the bedraggled woman-child that entered the Pinola village that fateful night, and tearfully betrayed her evil father Zekod and her two brothers. She endured deep anguish and a scarred soul when the Pinola council exiled her mother and brothers. Aleeta's mother, banished forever, spewed venomous words at her. Uri was troubled that this might damage Aleeta's life permanently. If it had not been for him, Denar, and others who took her into their homes, Uri's concern would have come true.

Right after that nightmare took place Coran and Uri brought her to Dombara land. Her life began to transform. She reunited with her foster brother, Jai, who introduced her to a family that cared and wanted her. Most important, love entered her life.

Aleeta reached the front of the crowd of people assembled for the union. She took her place next to the priest, Elari. The crowd parted again, and through it walked Uri's

14

cousin, Coran. He wore the ceremonial blue robe of a Dombara priest. On his head was a simple headdress made of seashells and bright colored feathers. He took long steps up to where Aleeta stood. Tears beaded up in Coran's bright orange eyes. Most of the village was aware of how Coran remained beside her with love and patience, as she struggled through those tough times. Uri heard sniffles passing through the crowd.

Aleeta and Coran, lead by Elari, exchanged a few words, pledging themselves to stay faithful to each other while they learned the ancient rites for marriage. It was finished and everyone cheered. Uri happily joined the group of men congratulating Coran. Cheers and whoops of joy echoed around them. Uri peeked to see if he could see Luwanna in the crowd clustered by Aleeta. They were moving back to the edge of the trees. He saw an eruption of brightly colored beads showered down in the center of the women and girls. Uri smiled and brought his attention back to Coran, whose friends now pushed him toward the tables of food that was prepared for this happy event.

In spite of the gaiety and joy taking place in the peaceful, evening air, sinister plans were unfolding. A dark figure watched in the bushes and trees at the edge of the play field, next to where the girls giggled and threw beads everywhere. He crouched low and crept forward. Moving closer... ever closer. His eyes were not wet with joy. Instead, they crinkled at the edges with glee. He was not invited, but he planned to take an important part in the celebration. He wouldn't share in the food, but his mouth watered at the deed he was about to perform. In his hand, he carried a cloth, damp with a liquid Master Tau had sold to him. It promised to cause immediate unconsciousness, without harming the intended victim.

The girls ran back to the group and left Aleeta to pick up the colored beads. She began to hum happily, as she emptied one handful after another into her pocket.

It was time for Rill to make his move.

xxx

Uri joined the group of men surrounding Coran. The men ceremoniously dumped barrels of flower petals and berries on Coran's head.

"No... no!" Hollered Coran and they doubled over with laughter.

Food began to leave the tables and appeared on plates as everyone settled down to eat.

Music floated over the group and Uri grabbed Luwanna's hand. She laughed and together they moved in circles to the rhythm of the music.

"I'm hungry." Luwanna said. "Let's get some food before it's all gone."

"You've always had a good appetite." Uri teased as they circled in the direction of the tables.

They saw Coran standing still, all alone. Uri thought it was strange Aleeta had not gotten back from the edge of the play field with the rest of the young women.

"Where is Aleeta?" Coran looked into the crowd, as he began to moved back and forth in an agitated manner. "Have you seen her?" He asked a group of her friends.

"No, the last time we saw her we were with her by the edge of the park. We showered her with the beads and then we all ran over here to the tables." Lyshon said.

A murmur spread quickly as one by one people acknowledged she was not among them. Uri grew alarmed. Coran began to run through the crowd and out the edges of the park. Soon everyone was running in different directions to the outskirts of the grass, calling her name.

Aleeta was gone. She had vanished like a whisper of smoke.

Coran ran to Uri and grabbed him hard by the shoulders, his tears flowed like great rivers. "Oh my Lord, please no! He must have her. It's the only explanation."

Uri's mouth flew open, suddenly understanding what Coran meant.. *No, not that. Please… not that.*

"Hurry," cried Elajon "We must form groups of searchers to scour the brush and forest. Quickly grab the lanterns and the torches!"

In a flash, the men armed with most of the available lights, started to trample through the brush along the play field and out into the forest beyond.

The women began to clean up the trays of food and debris from the festivities. They wept, frightened, confused, and stayed close to each other. An evening that had started bright and beautiful had now turned dark and menacing. A cloud covered the moons and a shadow came over the whole assemblage. How quickly cries of joy were replaced by cries of fear.

Chapter Four

The Gatherer

Rill's heart beat quickened as he observed the crowd of females turn to run back to the men while leaving Aleeta alone to pick up the beads on the ground. He sprung into action and in an instant she was his, her mouth and nose covered with the damp cloth. He looked into her beautiful eyes, wide and full of fear. He watched those eyes close as she drifted into unconsciousness. The sinister glee on his face spread out and widened his already full, puffy features.

"Don't worry my dear. I will not hurt you. You are much too precious to harm. However, we will be going on a long journey together." He talked as he worked, quickly covering her eyes and mouth with a rough cloth, and tying her hands and ankles. When finished and he seemed satisfied with the knots, he carried her over to his noogan and laid her gently in front of his seat.

Noogans were an amazing animal. Stocky, wide, and muscular, they could carry an enormous amount of weight. This was an animal not only good in the trees and brush, but able to transport heavy burdens through unusual locations. The mottled color of their fur blended into most any type of background. Their hooves were so flexible they would flatten out for sandy trails, or mold onto uneven rocky terrain. These animals could travel anywhere, and were perfectly capable for the journey ahead.

The noogan trotted along, carrying Rill and the unconscious Aleeta. He hurried into the trees to the back of the village and before she was missed they traveled far enough away so no one from the gathering would find them. Soon they would be far away to the east, where Rill believed the Dombaras would not think of looking.

His body in tune with the swaying of the animal, Rill congratulated himself on how patient he had become. Waiting through the ceremony, while knowing soon all that happiness would turn to anguish and fear, produced one of the greatest pleasures of his life. As Aleeta and the other girls came closer and closer throwing those colored beads, the anticipation of capturing her created a shiver of joy throughout his body. He recognized Luwanna and little Sarella with the group. He wished he could grab them all at once, but he had to control his impulses.

Capturing young maidens required Rill to develop patience and control of his impulses. While living many months in the Dombara Land, and visiting the Umbinga Tribe, he perfected this skill. Rill had a core of violence and sadism that made him perfect for this task, and mastering control of that violence made him twice as dangerous. He reveled in the thrill of stalking, and watching the look in their eyes as they realized they were in deep trouble. Here, Rill was in his element.

Dree, the boy who had saved his life, introduced to him to the oris root to take away his headaches. However it left Rill with an addiction that lead him to do whatever it took to obtain the drug directly from the Umbinga tribe. They always needed young maidens to do the field work and household work. The tribe wouldn't explain why, but he didn't much care anyway. The drug was the only thing on his mind.

He moved in unison with the noogan, sitting behind his prize capture, and together they trotted off in the direction of the eastern trails.

xxx

Aleeta became aware of lying on the cold ground. Her head buzzed and everything she looked at was out of focus. The rough cloth that covered her eyes was irritating, but when Aleeta tried to rub them, she discovered her hands tightly bound behind her. She tried to talk, but nothing would come out. Aleeta squirmed, and attempted to cry through the gag.

Rill looked over and saw that his prize had regained her senses. He knelt down beside her, and removed the cloths. "Don't tire yourself my sweet." Rill cooed in her ear. "No one can hear you. By now we are far away."

As her eyes began to move in unison, she made out a figure in front of her. He opened a door to a small, low hut. She looked around and saw they were deep in the forest. She opened her mouth to speak again, and her voice came out shaking and squeaky, but she continued. "Rill, what are you doing?"

"Oh really... you know what is happening. The big, bad Rill got you." He came over to her and put his face close to hers. "Uri must have told you what a bad boy I am."

"I don't need Uri to tell me about you. I remember you when you hung out with my brothers. Why did you take me away? Do you hate Coran and Uri that much?"

"Ah, I don't care about Coran." He stood up, "Now Uri, I hate him more than life."

"Why."

Rill helped her to stand and removed the ropes. Then he shoved her into the dark, smelly hut.

20

"Don't you know?" Rill stood by the open door, framed by the night's feeble light. His figure hunched over because of the low ceiling. "He tried to kill me. He left me in the Green Sea to die during a terrible storm. However, I didn't die. I hung on to what was left of the boat for hours, days."

Aleeta watched his eyes take on a wild, angry glow.

"Then the boy Dree found me and saved my life. Uri not only tried to kill me." he came close, standing toe to toe with her. "He murdered my mother."

"I don't believe that!" Aleeta cried out.

"Oh.. it's true. He knew the Dombaras were coming. They took us away in the middle of the night to the Dombara land. He met Bibbi in the desert, and I know Uri told them how to capture us."

Aleeta backed away, terrified of this maniac in front of her. Every fiber of her body posed, prepared to flee. However, his body denied her access to the door.

"My mother was sick and needed me to help her. Because of Uri, she died. He will get what's coming to him. I'll see to that." Then he turned and left the hut, closing the door behind him.

Aleeta tried to make sense of his ramblings. She had heard the story of Uri being lost at sea. She knew of the kidnappings of all the Pinola children, and the secret that they were really Dombara children. Her brother Jai was one. She knew what he was talking about, but she didn't understand why he thought Uri was responsible for it all. Why did Rill think Uri tried to kill him? Again, Aleeta struggled for the reason as to why he had abducted her. "He must be mad." She whispered to herself. "Oh please Lord, protect me from this crazy man."

21

Chapter Five
Safe Keeping

Uri ran through the women looking for Luwanna. At last, he spotted her. Uri grabbed her by the shoulders. "I got scared when I couldn't see you."

Luwanna said, "Uri, do you think...?"

"Yes, it has to be. He has had a long time to arrange this, and I'm sure his plan is clever."

"Will they find them?" Luwanna tried to hold back her tears.

Uri didn't answer. He held her in his arms. "You must be very careful. You know how much Rill wants to take you."

"Don't leave me. I thought I would never be frightened of him. Now I see how he operates. He is like a ghost...in and out, without anyone seeing anything."

"I will not leave your side." Uri promised. They moved over to a bench and sat down. "Everyone is wasting time looking for him in the forest to the west. Rill will be back in this area."

"Poor Coran. He must be frantic." Luwanna wiped the wetness from her face.

"Rill has changed since we all were taken to Dombara Land. Then he was only a bully. The last three years he has learned how to hate with patience and purpose." Uri said quietly. "He has learned to harness all the energy used for throwing fits of temper. Now he plans his moves with precision. He knows what he is doing and how to go about achieving what he wants."

"But it is still all about him. Rill thinks he is so very shrewd, and smarter than anyone else." Luwanna sighed deeply.

"We know where he eventually will be headed. The same place he took the Mountain People's women"

"He will be headed south of Bast area." Luwanna nodded. "But we have never been there. How can we trace his steps in an area we don't know anything about?"

"Again, we must trust The Creator. However, I don't want to be going after you, too." Uri looked very seriously at her. "I promised I would never leave you, but we both know I cannot stay close to you all day and night. We must have someone that can be with you when you are not with me."

"Tareen can come and stay with me. School is out and I will ask her…"

"No," Uri shook his head. "That would be an invitation for Rill to grab both of you. What about your grandmother? She's a feisty old gal, and has lots of close neighbors."

"Yes, that is a good idea. She is fun, and if anyone got close to me, she would flatten him. Let's go ask her now."

Uri knew Luwanna and Lyshon's grandmother, Prisea, well. She lived near the docks.

Prisea owned a medium size boat, and could out-fish most of the men. She sustained herself making and selling

23

woven baskets. Her modest home, located near the busy market place, would be safe for Luwanna. She could learn many things besides helping her grandmother. Prisea's daily chores included various methods of living off the land. It was an ideal place for Luwanna to spend the summer.

"I noticed Prisea wasn't at the betrothal celebration?" Uri remarked as they walked down the path to the sea shore.

"No. She injured her neck many years ago and suffers from pain, most of the time. She chose to attend the wedding over the betrothal."

Uri turned and looked at Luwanna. "Is she able to protect you with this disability?"

"Pain does not hinder someone from being strong and forceful." Luwanna answered."I know from experience."

As Uri and Luwanna approached her home, a small, sturdy woman appeared in the doorway, smiled, and opened her arms for Luwanna.

"My dear, what a surprise." Her hair, speckled with grey, swirled about her head, held high with a sparkling shell comb. Her pleasant face shone with happiness at the sight of Luwanna. "Have you returned from the celebration?"

"Marmie, something terrible happened." Luwanna began. "Aleeta has disappeared."

"What do you mean...disappeared?" Prisea asked.

Luwanna began to cry. "She was with us, and we were throwing strings of beads at her. When we went back to the tables, she wasn't with us any more."

Prisea looked to Uri for more details.

"There is someone kidnapping young women. He has done this to the Bast and the Mountain People for many months. You don't know him, but he is a Dombara, my age. However, he lives and dresses as a Bast."

Luwanna grabbed Prisea's hand. "Marmie, remember when I told you about Uri and a boy named Rill, escaping back to Pinola Land?"

Prisea nodded

"Rill is the person we are talking about."

Uri sighed. "He is very evil, perhaps even mad. He hates me with a deep passion, and he wants to get Luwanna. Can she stay here until he is caught, or at the very least gone? She must be around someone every moment of the day and night. Believe me, she's in great danger."

"Yes, I will protect her. If he comes around here he will regret it." She firmly stuck her chin out, and her eyes narrowed. "No one will harm my honey girl, if I'm around."

"Thank you," Uri said. "I feel much better. I can't stay with her all the time so I'm relieved to know she will be safe."

Pointing to the chairs by the front of her house, Prisea said. "Let's sit down."

They pulled the chairs close together and Prisea continued. "Are the men searching for Aleeta?"

"Yes, they have spread out and have gone into the bushes and forest around the area. I know Rill. He has planned this well and has taken Aleeta nowhere near. When he leaves, if they haven't found her, they will have to follow him into the southern part of Dombara Land, past the Bast Village. It is a long way. None of us have ever gone there before."

The old woman waggled her finger. "Ah… I have heard of a land far way. Beyond the cold mountains where rain turns

25

white and covers the hills. I have heard that strange people live there."

"Why would anyone want to live where it is so cold?" Luwanna asked.

"These stories are only pieces of rumors and myths, my dear." Prisea said.

Uri was interested. "What about these people? Do you know anything else?"

"The stories are very old. They live in tall structures with many rooms. Whole families live together. The story goes; their women are for childbearing only. They treat them as if they are goddesses. The men use female slaves for all the household duties, and attending to their wives, and the slaves also raise the children... so the legend goes."

"We have never heard of such things in Pinola Land." Uri commented.

"The people of Pinola Land isolated themselves from the rest of our world. They kept it that way for eons. Now that you have opened it to the new ways, and the knowledge of The Creator, it will be both a blessing and a curse." Prisea said with sadness in her voice.

"What do you mean, Marmie?" Luwanna asked.

"When we open ourselves up to knowledge of any kind, good and bad comes together. The Pinola's will eventually learn of their history and of ours. There will be many surprises along the way."

Uri listen carefully to what the old woman said, believing there was much wisdom and truth in the old tales. He knew that Rill dealt with a people that lived far south. He obtained women for these people. Were they the slaves? Then Uri remembered Aleeta had mentioned her father was going to sell her as a slave. Uri realized Rill must receive something he greatly desires for bringing these young women to this tribe.

By the time Uri left Luwanna at her grandmother's home, it was very late. Leaving the cozy home, with golden lights dancing in the front windows, was difficult. However, he made his way down the path to his house.

It was quiet... Sarella was sleeping, but he noticed a dim light peeking from the crack of his mother's bedroom door. He knew she was waiting for Elajon to return home. The men wouldn't search much longer tonight. There would be preparations for a long and exhausting trip, deep into the southern part of the land tomorrow. Maybe if they moved along with speed, they could over take Rill on the trail. Uri decided he would not take part in this search. He was determined to stay close to Luwanna. It was probable that Rill would return for her as well.

Chapter Six
Alone

Aleeta woke with a start. The sun shone through the cracks in the roof at a steep angle telling the tale of early morning.

It took a moment to remember where she was, and she began to tremble. She hurt all over. They must have crossed a lot of rough terrain on the noogan. Her eyes were still irritated from the coarse, dirty cloth used to cover them before they began their trip, and she rubbed them again.

Rill had dumped her in this shack after he untied her hands and feet. It was so dark she could hardly see a thing. When he came back after leaving for a few minutes, he caught her looking for an opening.

"Oh, my dear, you mustn't try to move around. I don't want to hurt you." He patted her face. "Precious cargo."

She moved away from his touch, but he pulled her toward him again and stared menacingly into her eyes. After a long moment, Rill pushed her back against the wall. He took a long rope from his pocket and tied one end around a hook attached to the wall. Next, he wrapped the rope around her ankle. She tried to pull her leg away, but he had a tight grip on her. Making a thick knot, he grinned. "Just for security, my dear. You have plenty of room to move about." He left once again, leaving her in the shack alone. She heard a bar drop outside, locking her in.

She rocked and moaned to herself for hours. It was late into the night when she finally fell asleep.

Now she was awake, hungry, and angry. Now that it was light, Aleeta studied her surroundings. Rill had put together a small log shelter. He must have used material that was in the area, she reasoned. There was a door, but no windows. She looked down at the ragged mat she had slept on and shuddered. The floor consisted of smooth dirt.

As she thought of digging through the floor under the logs, the door flew open. The sun blinded Aleeta as it shone in, and she covered her eyes. Blinking several times, she began to focus in on the figure of Rill standing over her.

"Mornin' my sweet. Did you have a nice restful sleep?"

His voice caused her stomach to flip and she fought the nausea that welled up inside.

"I hope you like your home here. In another day or so, you will have company. Then we will set out on a long voyage."

He squatted down in front of her. His fingers reached out and brushed her hair off her face. Aleeta recoiled from his touch, suppressing the desire to bite his hand as hard as possible.

He bent closer. "I see in your eyes a fierce anger." His breath was foul. She looked into his face, hoping to see some compassion she could appeal to, but saw emptiness. There was no emotion, none. Aleeta scooted back from him.

"I think I will wait to get your breakfast. That should humble you a bit." Rill grimaced.

Aleeta thought, *"Give me breakfast and I'll throw it in your face."* However, she kept her thoughts to herself.

"Make yourself comfortable." Rill chuckled. He put a jar of water within her reach.

"Why are you doing this?" Aleeta asked. "You know everyone will be searching for me."

A faint smile played with the corners of his mouth. He touched his lip with his tongue.

"Ha...ha. Have a nice day. See you soon."

The door shut and she was in shadows once again.

What was happening? She strained to remember how she got here. The last thing she remembered were the girls throwing colored beads at her. As she was picking them off the ground, everything went black. She quickly reached into her large pocket to feel those beads buried deep inside. Yes, they were there, and she thought of a plan to using them, and maybe save her from this lunatic.

"I can't sit here and do nothing," she thought, and rubbed her ankle where the rope began to make a sore over the anklebone. She scooted to the door and pounded on it. Screaming, she pounded on all the walls. Then she began pushing and pulling for a loose log or anything, she could pry up and escape. She kept up until her hands became bruised and bloody. After a long time, exhausted, she went over to a corner and sat sobbing. Again, the thought of digging through to the outside played with her mind. Aleeta looked at her thin fingers and decided she was incapable of succeeding at that task.

The day seemed endless, the longest day of her life. Aleeta tried to remember all the Holy Writings she had learned. She repeated prayers to The Creator of All. She asked Him why He allowed this nightmare. Aleeta believed her life would now become a happy one. She dreamed of being with Coran forever. Loving, laughing, and growing old with him. Now she wondered, is this dream over or just postponed?

Finally, darkness crept into the hut. She shivered from the cold. There was no relief from the wretched conditions. When the darkness was complete, Rill came in. In silence, he handed her a biscuit and some dried chewy meat. It was the first food she had seen all day.

He yawned and lay on the mat. Aleeta was glad he left her alone, however now she had to listen to his incessant snoring. She scooted up against her corner and covered her feet with her dress. It was nothing new to sleep sitting in an upright position. Aleeta had done it before.

When Rill woke in the morning, he brewed some crost and brought her a grimy cup, half-full, and another biscuit. A strange look came over his face as he began to leave. His eyes narrowed and his nose wrinkled. The corners of his jaws tightened as he spoke to Aleeta through his teeth. "I'll get her tonight night. Yes, I will."

He left Aleeta to face another miserable day, hungry and aching from head to toe. She got up and went to the door, dragging the rope behind her, but found it locked again. She screamed until her throat hurt, hoping someone would hear her. She paced back and forth most of the day, several times she thought her mind was leaving her body. She drank all the stale water, and by evening, she was huddled again in a corner, weeping until no more tears would come.

Chapter Seven
Preparations

Uri leaped out of bed. The sun shining through the bedroom window told him it was midmorning. He went to the kitchen where Elajon sat at the table. Deep circles pocketed his eyes, and an aura of defeat enveloped him.

"How did it go?" Uri asked, referring to the night search. He sat across from his father and reached for a piece of fruit from the bowl that perpetually sat in the center of the table.

"Not well. We could not find any trace of them. It was like they just vanished...poof."

"Maybe you couldn't find any tracks, because they are still in the area." As Uri heard his own words, a slow chill crawled up his back. "Maybe Rill isn't done." He whispered.

"I got about three hours of sleep." Elajon moaned. "It is so discouraging. Coran is devastated."

"I need to go visit with him." Uri stood. "Try to relax and eat something."

Elajon nodded.

Uri walked over to the huts the village had built for Coran and Aleeta. His cousin sat by the front door. Uri approached slowly, studying his expression. Coran's posture radiated pain, but there was a fire of determination emanating from his eyes.

"Hello." Coran greeted Uri.

"How are you holding up?" Uri asked.

"I am numb. I don't feel anything. I won't think how life would be without Aleeta. If Rill has taken her, I pray he will treat her well. She is strong and has been through fire before, plus she has deep faith. I know she will come through this, also. However, they could be miles away by now." Coran brushed away his tears.

"I think you can be assured, they are still close by."

"What makes you say that?" Coran looked up.

"'Rill is still here because he is not finished adding to his collection. I believe he will try to take Luwanna next."

"That may be right, but I pray not." There was a long pause. "Now I must wait."

"When Rill begins to move we will follow him." Uri offered hope.

Coran looked at Uri. The corners of his mouth turned down and in a low voice, he warned. "I agree with you. Watch Luwanna. She is the key."

Uri suddenly felt nauseous. "Have you had a vision?" he whispered.

"No."

"I think I might have." Uri confessed. "But it was all mixed up and I think visions are very clear, am I right?"

"Yes, there is no mistaking their meaning."

Unnerved by Coran's ominous warnings, Uri left and went directly to Prisea's home. His feet could not move fast enough. When he reached the house, he breathed a sigh of relief. The two of them sat outside, cutting up vegetables.

Luwanna jumped up to meet him. "Have you heard anything? Did they find…"

"No, we think Rill is still in the area." Uri said trying to hide the concern in his voice.

"Did you remember tomorrow is the welcome home party for Tika and Koori?" Luwanna reminded him.

"Oh, that's right." he sighed. "They will be arriving late this afternoon."

Their replacement left Dombara Land to sail across the Green Sea a week ago. After a few days of training and familiarizing themselves with the people and the land, the couple would take over Koori and Tika's position. They would help shepherd the believers along with Denar, his wife, and another Dombara couple. Rotating the Dombara people seemed to work well. No one suffered a burnout, and in several months refreshed, Koori and Tika would return to relieve another couple.

Elajon did not cancel their welcome home party. He thought it would help divert everyone from mourning over Aleeta's disappearance.

Late in the afternoon of the next day, the party began. Not as many people were there as invited, but that was to be expected. Marga and Koori's mother, Ribha, had cooked and prepared a large quantity of food, however no one seem hungry.

Uri moved though the guests numb, and distracted. There was a damp cloud of concern over what should have been a joyous occasion. Marga occupied herself playing with the baby Ranui. He squealed with delight as she chased him around the room.

Bibbi stayed by Uri and hugged his arm. "I am afraid. Is it normal to feel that way?"

"Of course it is." Uri's voice was barely above a whisper.

"Can I go with you to help find Aleeta?" Bibbi asked.

"Bibbi, you are only ten. You know you are too young to join a rescue group. You would hinder more than help. You don't want to do that, do you?"

"No...I want to help somehow."

"You can pray. Aleeta needs your prayers."

"Oh, I can do that." Bibbi nodded, satisfied.

As soon as Koori could wrest himself free from the guests, he came over to Uri.

"What is being done to find Aleeta? Elajon doesn't want to upset anyone by talking about it, so he has told us very little."

"Father has been one of the front leaders, but is exhausted, and needs rest. I'll fill you in." Uri led Koori outside to the front yard, where they could talk without interruption. He related the facts from the time Aleeta went missing "Rill is still in the area. They began looking down the trails, but they weren't able to find any tracks."

"Have they looked in the caves around the shore line?"

"Yes, and they found nothing. Listen, I believe he is still here because he wants Luwanna, and is waiting for an opportunity to grab her."

"Why? Why is he doing this?" Koori shook his head.

"Last year when I was here, we hunted for Zekod. After he was killed and we escaped from the Bast Tribe, we came back through the mountains and met the people that live in the hills to the west." Uri explained. "They recently had two young women disappear. It appears Rill is taking young women to a tribe far to the south, and he is getting something in return. I don't know what."

"What matters is where Aleeta is now." Korri rubbed his chin. "However, what will Rill do if he is unable to capture Luwanna?"

"I don't think he will leave until he does. My hope is we can catch him trying." Uri peered into the front room. He looked for the face of Luwanna, and spotted her in a group surrounding Tika.

"He has had a long time to set this up and I'm sure he is being very careful." Uri looked back at Koori. "Let's go back inside and try to enjoy the party."

xxx

As the sun went behind the trees, Rill took soot from the dead fire pit he used to warm himself during the long evenings, and blackened his face and arms. He pulled a dark woven cap over his head. Now he would blend in with the darkness of the night.

His heart pounded with anticipation, and he briefly thought of taking a small chew of the root, only to calm him down. But no, he needed all his senses sharp tonight.

He began to walk toward the village and Uri's hut. He could tell something special was going on because of all the lights. Rill was certain the villagers were planning to search for Aleeta, but this seemed more like a party.

Peeking through the trees, he saw Tika and Marga near a window, but he wasn't interested in them. He crept closer and neared the front. There she was, with Uri. Ah, she would have to go home sometime tonight. Travel down the path, in the blackness of night.

Rill knew every inch of that trail from Uri's hut, where the shadows from the trees consumed the light, and where they would come upon the darkest area. He snickered. It would be so easy, and right under Uri's nose.

Chapter Eight

Disaster

The blackness enveloped the land like a heavy blanket. The moon Venca was yet to rise, but Visca, in its waning phase, hovered over the inky land and shone weakly between the clouds that veiled the black canopy. When the clouds completely covered the moon, no eye could capture enough light to see more than a yard away. Maybe not even that far.

Uri sat with Luwanna outside the house where people still milled about, talking quietly. He wanted to hold her hand, but couldn't get up the courage. They had been sitting there for an hour, chattering away as usual. Talking about the past, the years they grew up together in Pinola Land, and the adjustment to the different life with the Dombaras. They reminisced about the adventure to the Land of the Bast. There was so much to talk about, so many years of friendship. Uri had been gone this last year, finishing school in the Pinola village, so it had been a while since they had a chance to just sit and chat. He noticed how she had changed, more delicate and soft, more woman-like.

His feelings toward her had evolved. When she was very young, he was like an older brother. Then she became a good friend, but now his heart leapt when he first saw her a week ago after he arrived from Pinola Land. What was happening? Surely, he couldn't be feeling love, in a man and woman way, could he? He was only seventeen, soon to be eighteen, and she much younger, only sixteen. However, the thought of her not being in his life was too painful to imagine. He sighed and clasped his hands together. Now was not the time for such ideas. He had to decide what he wanted to do with his life, and there was this ugly business with Rill to deal with.

"Is there something wrong?" Luwanna asked, sensing Uri's anxiety.

"No."

"I must start for home." She stated flatly. "It is getting really late."

"You should stay here until morning." Uri said.

"I can't. Marmie would be frantic if I don't come home."

"Oh... yes, of course." Uri lit a torch and stood at the end of the steps as he waited for her to say her goodbyes to Tika and Koori, and then they began walking down the path. It was so dark he could hardly see her or the trail. "Stay close to me." he warned Luwanna, knowing they were still near the trees and brush. "Hold my hand. It is very dark."

The light from the torch flickered dimly onto the pathway.

"I know where I am. I'm fine." She reassured him. They walked a while in uncomfortable silence.

"What's wrong, Uri?" Luwanna asked again. "You have been very quiet tonight."

"It frightens me to know Rill hasn't given up on taking you away." Uri thought about the threat before they left the Bast land. Rill tried then, and said he would not stop until he captured her. Rill knew any attack on Luwanna would devastate Uri.

"It could happen anytime." Uri took his eyes off Luwanna for a second watching the clouds thicken over the moon. He looked back, squinting in order to see a shadow where he thought Luwanna should be. Uri hardly felt the thud on the back of his head and he fell unconscious to the ground. The clouds obscured the moon completely.

xxx

The world began to appear as a small spot, fuzzy and whirling. The spot began to grow bigger. Uri's hand went to the pain on the back of his head and with a jolt he winced as he felt a small lump.

"Luwanna, where are you?" His voice came out squeaky. Uri shook his head and tried to speak again. "Luwanna!" He struggled to sit up as he reached out for the torch on the ground. The torch flickered dimly, but he grabbed onto it tightly. Panic set in. "Luwanna!" He screamed.

It was unbelievable. While they discussed the event, it had happened. He couldn't breathe. He felt his heart stop and get caught in his throat. Grasping out like a blind man, Uri stumbled aimlessly in the bushes, bumping into a tree. He fell to his knees and a thunderous groan emitted from the depth of his being. The sound resounded high into the night air. She was gone. Rill had come up behind him and hit him on the head, and made off with her.

The clouds passed and the moon once again dimly lit up the path and the brush around him. He had heard nothing, felt nothing, saw nothing. Rill was like a ghost. He came and went without a sound. Uri was supposed to protect her. In a split second, he failed. Somehow, Rill attained what he was after, and right under Uri's nose. He was not sure what to do next. Uri turned with the burned out torch clutched in his hand, and ran for home. By the time he ran into the living area, he was hysterical. Sobs and groans fell from his lips, and tears blinded him. Everyone that still lingered at the party surrounded him. Uri saw their lips move and the concern in their eyes, but he was not able to hear anything. All he was able to do was blurt out that Rill had taken Luwanna.

"I failed to protect her." He sobbed and fell helplessly in a heap on the floor. The sound of his own voice brought back his hearing and he again could breathe normally.

"Hold it together. This isn't helping." Elajon shook Uri by the shoulders.

He looked up into his father's eyes. "Please, we have to find her right away."

Coran took Uri's face in his large hands. "That is how I felt, but we must not rush out and go off in a panic. We know Rill has them. He has a plan, so we must have one too."

Uri coughed and blinked, attempting to control himself, and think rationally. "Now he will begin to leave the area and also leave behind tracks."

"That's right. We now will have tracks to follow." Coran agreed.

"Abosol!" Uri jumped to his feet. "We need Abosol."

"Good idea." Coran returned Uri's excitement.

"Who is Abosol?" Elajon asked.

Coran looked from Uri to Elajon. "He is a Pinola, renown for his tracking abilities. Abosol tracked for us when we went to find what Zekod and his bunch were involved in."

"Abosol is strong and a steady believer of The Way." Uri added. "I have the utmost trust and belief in him. With his skills I know we will find the girls."

"How soon can he get here?" Elajon questioned.

Coran said "If I leave right way, I could be back here with him by tomorrow night."

Elajon took a deep breath, relieved to see something could be done. "Well, let's get you on your way."

It didn't take long for them to help Coran prepare for the trip across the Green Sea. They made their way down to the shore where Elajon offered a prayer as Coran climbed aboard the small boat.

"Lord, Creator of All, calm the sea and protect your servant, Coran as he crosses over to Pinola Land. Bless Abosol and all the men who begin the dangerous hunt for this vicious man who has abducted your two precious children."

Elajon put his arm over Uri's shoulder as they watched the boat leave the docks and head into the night. Anger and grief again clasped onto Uri's heart. Above the small group standing by the water, two moons shone weakly, and Uri felt the calming cool breeze. He said his own silent prayer for Luwanna, and released her into the protective arms of The Creator.

Chapter Nine
Aleeta Gets Company

Consciousness returned slowly to Luwanna. The first thing she noticed were the scratchy strips that covered her mouth and eyes, the second thing, her hands tied tightly behind her. In addition, the back of her head hurt. Not far away an animal brayed. Then Luwanna heard a voice she knew all too well.

"Awake already? That's too bad. You won't enjoy the ride much." She felt Rill lift her and put her over the back of an animal. The pungent smell overwhelmed her and she tried to cough, but gagged instead. . Luwanna's belly lay flat against the animal's backside, her tied hands dangled below her on one side of the animal and her legs on the other. Slowly her feet grew numb. How more uncomfortable could she get? Rill leapt on behind her, and as they started to move, she began to feel the answer to that question. The movement of the animal hurt every muscle in her body.

The bumpy, painful ride seemed to go on forever. Finally they stopped. Luwanna felt Rill jump to the ground and lift her off the noogan. Unable to stand, she fell to the ground while the pain in her feet worsened as circulation returned.

He untied the cloths from her eyes and mouth, but the faint light of the moons above gave her little comfort, and she blinked.

"We are here." Rill cocked his head and looked blankly at her.

She turned, and in front of her squatted a small, wooden structure. The workmanship was inferior to anything she had seen. It sagged to the left and mud mixed with grass covered the roof. It reminded Luwanna the way the Mudans built their homes. However, the Mudans had perfected the mud and grass combination, and their huts were sturdy and large. Rill lifted her to her feet, and dragging her, she stumbled to the door. When he opened it, Luwanna gasped and let out a cry. She saw Aleeta lying on the floor. "You are alive! Oh thank you, my dear Lord."

"Of course she's alive." Rill snickered. "You two precious girls are worth a small fortune." He led Luwanna in through the door, and untied her hands. She fell on Aleeta, hugged her, and covered her with kisses.

Rill continued pleasantly. "I will take good care of you both. In fact I even brought you some food." He strutted out to the noogan and removed a pack. He entered the hut with a package wrapped in the large leaves of the Tobanyant tree. "Here," he handed it to Luwanna.

She removed the leaves, revealing generous portion of fruit and vegetables. Included were sweet cakes. Luwanna recognized them from her grandmother's kitchen. "You rotten thief!" She screamed at Rill "You entered my marmie's house and stole these from her."

"I am sure she would want you to have them. Especially under the circumstances." Rill began to laugh. It turned into a cackle. "So eat hardy, my darlin's. Tomorrow, before dawn, we are leaving." He left the hut to tend to the animal.

Luwanna pushed her share of food over to Aleeta. "Take my share, I'm not hungry."

Aleeta began to fill her mouth. "I'm starving."

Luwanna knew she could go a long time with very little food. Aleeta was thin and on the frail side, so Luwanna had to be sure she got enough to eat and plenty of rest.

"Your hands are bruised. Did he..."

"No, I did it myself, trying to get out of here." Aleeta said, her mouth full.

"From the outside it looks as though it would fall over easily."

"Believe me; it is sturdier than it looks." Aleeta's hair hung in dirty strips in front of her face. Her beautiful dress was torn and smudged. Her feet were bare, and bruises circled where the rope continued to scuff up her ankle.

Luwanna was horrified at Aleeta's condition. If Aleeta could fall apart in just two days, Luwanna knew someone had to take care of her. Luwanna had no way of knowing how far they would travel, or where. She had no idea of how long it would take a rescue party to reach them.

"Well," Luwanna said, "I am sure of one thing. Eventually we will be found."

Aleeta felt better now that she had food in her belly. "Is Coran okay?"

"He is holding up. The men believed that Rill stayed in the area to go after me. As you can see, they were right. Maybe a group will start out in the morning or maybe the next day. It will be a while before they find the trail." Luwanna sighed wearily. "Don't worry, Aleeta. They won't give up until they find us."

They huddled close to together and comforted each other as the night wore on.

Luwanna woke as dawn filled the sky with the promise of another day. She looked over at Aleeta, curled into a tight ball beside her. The hut was faintly lit from a lantern on the floor, however Rill had stayed out of sight all night.

She began to hear noises from outside. He said they were leaving early in the morning. Where, she wondered, would they be taken next?

Aleeta moaned and rolled over on her back. With slow and quiet movements, Luwanna crept along the floor to the door and peeked through a small crack. She saw the noogan standing still and packed to the hilt. Then Rill came into view. He was busy fiddling with water bags.

Luwanna crawled back to Aleeta. "Wake up." She gently shook her.

Aleeta opened her eyes and began to smile at Luwanna. She stretched and closed her eyes again.

"Aleeta, what's the matter with you? Wake up. Rill is getting ready to leave."

With that, Aleeta sat straight up. "Oh, I was having a wonderful dream. Coran and I were sitting on the shore of a beautiful blue lake."

"I'm sorry to disturb your dream, sweetie, but you need to get up and get ready for Rill's next move."

Tears brimmed in Aleeta's eyes. "Oh, I want to go home." She began to sob.

Luwanna wrapped her arms around the frail girl. "Me too, but we need to deal with what is happening right now."

Aleeta nodded, sniffed, and stood up.

At that moment, the door sprang open. Rill walked in. "Good mornin'. Ready for a long walk? I think you both can make it just fine."

"Where are we going?" Luwanna asked.

"South, to my home. That will be the first leg of the trip. So grab something to eat and let's go." He pushed the girls out the door and into the cool dampness of the morning.

Chapter Ten
Help From Across the Sea

Coran reached the Pinola shore just as dawn broke. He leapt out of the boat and grabbed the water jug. Food was out of the question. He had eaten very little since Aleeta disappeared. He silently began the dusty trek up the road. Abosol's hut sat at the outskirts of the village, just a few yards off the trail near the southern well. It didn't take very long to reach it and soon Coran was pounding on the roughly hewn door.

As the door opened, a hairy hulk blinked sleep from puffy eyes. "What do I see standing in my doorway? Is it a mirage?"

"What do I see, standing in your doorway? Is it animal or human?"

Abosol let out a gruff laugh. "Is it that bad? Come in and tell me what brings you here so early in the day."

As Abosol made a pot of crost, Coran related the past events to him.

"We need you to help us track down Rill and find the girls." He finished. "Tracking is the only way and hope we find them before Rill gets them too far south"

Abosol sat across from Coran. "What is the terrain like? Are the trails far, and are they clear?"

48

"It's rough, and we will need noogans to carry supplies. However the trails are clearly marked. If we have to go beyond into the mountains, it will be new territory. I have no idea what we will come up against. In any case, it will be a long trip." Coran said.

"Wait. Noogans? What are noogans?" Abosol frowned.

"They are domesticated pack animals, and can carry heavy loads. Rill uses them for traveling. I will show you what their footprints look like." He picked up a vegetable husk lying on the floor and made a crude drawing on the dirt floor. "They are larger than the kavacs or bameas, and very furry."

"How fast do they travel? Can a man keep up with them or do we have to ride them?"Abosol got up and poured the hot crost into large cups.

'We have to load them heavily with all of our supplies. Noogans can carry a lot, but that will slow them down, so—" Coran blew on the hot liquid then continued, "we will have to walk. Still, I think we can travel faster than Rill. He will have two uncooperative women to deal with."

"I will be honored to help you, but have to finish a job I started for one of the elders before we leave." Abasol said as he stood up. "It will take me just a few hours. If you like, grab your cup and come with me into the village. You can visit with our friend Denar, and meet our new Dombara leaders of the Way." Abosol stretched and grabbed his sandals. "Are you ready?"

Coran nodded and followed him out the door.

xxx

Uri woke to Bibbi bouncing on his bed. "Wake up, wake up. We have to start to prepare for the rescue. There is so much to do. You need to get up."

49

Uri rubbed his eyes. "What do you mean...we?"

"Come on, you need me to help you prepare."

"Really, why?" Uri grinned. He understood Bibbi's excitement. His little brother was at the threshold of growing up, and he wanted to be included with the adult activities.

"Aw, you know I can help." Bibbi pouted.

Uri jumped out of bed and slipped his sandals on. "I suppose you can. But don't get any ideas about coming with us."

"I know."

Uri was surprised when he entered the kitchen. It was buzzing with activity. Marga and Elajon were at the table sorting heaps of different foods into six piles.

"Well, it's about time." Jai greeted him.

"What's happening?" Uri frowned.

"We are preparing for your long journey." Elajon said.

"We must keep the search party small." Jai explained. "You, me, Coran, Abosol, Oden, maybe Bo."

Uri wondered why the Bast friend, Bo, would be included. Jai had anticipated Uri's question.

"Bo knows the Bast territory better than anyone."

"Don't forget Abosol can track better than anyone I know of, from both sides of the sea." Uri added. Sleep still clouded his thoughts so he poured himself a cup of hot crost. He took a big gulp and asked, "What's the plan?"

"We need to take as many supplies as possible." Jai began. "Dried meat, dried fruit, and ingredients to make biscuits over a fire. Water and crost powder." He refreshed his cup with the hot drink and sat across from Uri. " A change of clothing, bargaining materials."

"Like money or rare items?"

"Yes."

Uri thought he had missed some information Jai had. "Why, do you think we might need to trade a commodity with someone?"

"Maybe. The thought came into my head. It couldn't hurt." Jai said.

"I guess not." Uri admitted.

Jai was the same age as Uri. However, he had grown much taller and stockier. Jai had thick blonde hair that fell in attractive waves across his forehead. Also, his thinking was different. He was more outgoing, and intuitive, thinking of circumstances outside the boundaries of normal happpenstances.

"We will need a noogan for each one of us, to carry supplies." Jai continued.

"How can we all afford to buy that many noogans?" Uri interrupted.

"My brother Goth has donated six of them from his farm." Jai answered.

"That's very generous of him." Uri was impressed. He had heard that Goth and his wife, Luwanna's sister Lyshon, had a piece of property out of town, and raised several different farm animals. They had done very well and had become successful in their business.

"Have you figured out how to cross the Bast River?" Bibbi asked.

"The last time Coran spoke with Bo, he said the bridge has been left down." Uri said.

Elajon spoke up, "What does that mean?"

"The Bast have a retractable bridge for crossing the river. Usually they pull it up, and hide it after they cross back into their territory." Jai explained. "Lately it had been left down."

"Does that mean they are not as suspicious as before?" Elajon asked.

"I'm not sure." Jai said. "Since we crossed the river without their bridge, maybe they…"

Oden appeared at the open door. "May I join?" he raised his hand.

Uri still became irritated at his condescending manner. "Only if you want to put your life at risk for the next several weeks." He grumbled into his cup.

"Oh, that sounds like fun." Oden snickered and walked over to the table.

"Seriously boys," Elajon said. "Time is of the essence. Coran will be back soon and you must be prepared."

"We can pack up the noogans while we wait." Oden offered.

"That's a good idea." Jai shook his head. "Let's pack up the food first."

As they all got busy and began working together, Uri pulled Jai aside.

"Why does Oden need to come with us?" Uri whispered.

"He offered his expertise of the Bast territory." Jai answered.

"Oh... that is not needed." Uri said emphatically. "Especially if Bo comes with us."

"What is it between you two?" Jai narrowed his eyes and looked closely at Uri.

"He thinks he is better than the rest of us. Besides, I have seen him looking at Luwanna." Uri replied.

"So?"

"He has been talking to her a lot, like at the betrothal party." Uri squinted his eyes in anger. 'I don't trust him."

"Uri... Are you jealous?" Jai grinned.

Uri's answer was quick. "No, of course not, but, he isn't good for her."

"And who would be?" Jai cocked his head.

"Let's stay on the subject. Why do we need him?"

"Many men in the tribe have come forward, offering their help. Elajon and Pujim talked to all of them. Oden seemed to be the one they thought would make a difference. He does have many skills we need. Because he is a part Dombara and part Mudan, he thinks a bit differently than we do." Jai explained.

"For some reason that irritates me." Uri regretted the comment as soon as it was out of his mouth. "I shouldn't have said that."

Jai reached out with a finger, touched Uri's lips. "The tongue can be like fire. We must keep control over it. It can bless and curse, and only one of those comes from our Holy Creator"

"Jai you know me. It was only a reflection of how I am feeling at the moment. I need prayer in this area. But... there is something about Oden that doesn't feel right to me."

"Oden is our Creator's child and He loves him as He loves us. Try to look at Oden through the eyes of our Savior." Jai rubbed Uri's arm. "He is different and I understand how you feel, but shrug it off."

Uri nodded "I'll have to deal with my feelings." Inside Uri felt a vague sense of anxiety. There really was something not right about Oden. He felt it when the two of them penetrated deep into Bast territory together. He felt it when Oden killed Zekod, cold and without hesitation. Yes, that had saved his life. But Uri thought there might have been a better way. Besides, Oden seemed to enjoy it a bit too much.

It was late in the afternoon by the time Coran and Abosol arrived. They walked into the area where everyone was working. Coran began to introduce Abosol to everyone. Uri came up to him and wrapped his arms around the big, hairy man.

"I've missed you, my friend." Uri spoke into Abosol's ear.

"Same here. I didn't get to say goodbye when you left."

"It was sudden." Uri explained.

"So, tell me all about this problem." Abosol sat down.

It took time to explain it all. Then he and Uri examined the noogans, as Tika and Marga presented snacks.

"We need to finish packing up the noogans." Elajon said. "Each one of you has your own animal and the extra one is for Bo." Elajon questioned Coran about the weather south. Was it cooler? In addition, he expressed concern for warmer clothing.

"When we reach the southern part of the Bast Land, we will decide if we need warmer clothing. For now, we will take blankets made from the bamea's wool." Coran answered.

Uri gazed at everyone in the circle. He noticed Oden sat separate while they ate, and watched every move Abosol made. He was measuring him up. Why?

Chapter Eleven
On the Edge

Luwanna walked as if in a trance. She was beyond exhaustion, and her feet started to bleed about two miles back. Rill had to place Aleeta on the noogan or she would have fainted, hours ago.

"Ah," he announced. "We are here."

Luwanna gazed up. In front of her and saw a clearing. In the center was a hut. A very welcome sight. Suddenly she couldn't go any further and sank to her knees. A boy emerged from the hut. He was trembling and cowered as Rill walked up to him.

"Bring the women in." Rill ordered him, and continued to bellow at him for the next hour. Luwanna was shocked at the manner in which Rill treated him.

"Can't you make something edible for dinner? You stupid, mush head."

"You didn't bring me anything to cook." The boy whimpered.

Rill screamed at him. "Find something fool!" He picked up a whip made from saw tooth grass and struck the boy across the legs. Red streaks rose up immediately.

Luwanna couldn't stand the abuse any longer. "Wait," she spoke up. "I'll help him."

"Good luck. I doubt anyone can help." Rill lay back in his hammock.

Luwanna went over and grabbed the boy's hand. "What is your name?"

"Dree."

"Come with me Dree. I will find some vegetables and roots around the area. We will fix dinner together."

A look of relief spread across Dree's face.

As they worked together, Luwanna tried to gain information from Dree.

"Do you know where Rill is taking us?" She asked.

"There is a tribe, very far to the south. He will take you there."

"Why?"

Dree looked at the ground. "He will sell you to them."

The horror of this information crawled up her back like an evil spirit. She took a deep breath. "Will you help us escape?"

"I am afraid of Rill."

Luwanna sighed. She tried to understand his fear. Again, she prayed that Uri and the others would hurry and get here before they traveled on to this terrible tribe.

"What kind of people is Rill selling us to?" Luwanna asked.

"They are nice, I guess. They use young women like you to do all their work, and take care of their wives and children. I don't know much about them." He stopped short of saying anything else.

"How do you know of these people?"

"I met them a few years ago, by accident. They were hunting for food. I don't know why they came so far north. I gave them a kavac I owned and they gave me a root they called oris." Dree glanced back to the hut. "When I chewed and ate some of it, I felt great. So I followed them to get more. Then when I helped Rill out from the sea, I gave him some to help him... you know."

Luwanna nodded, but she didn't know.

"He wanted more so I brought him to their outpost and he made deals with them."

"You mean deals about selling them women?" she asked.

"Yes, among other things. They need material to make cloth."

"Where is this outpost, is it close by?"

"No." Dree shook his head. "It is a long way from here. You travel through the hills before you get to the meadows of their land. It is very cold there."

"Did you ever see Rill with a Pinola man?" Luwanna changed the subject.

"I know he had a boat that he used to sail over to Pinola Land. Sometimes he came back with an older Pinola man."

"Hmmm... Luwanna mulled over that information. "Did he hang around any of the Dombaras?"

"He would go into the village, at night. I didn't know what he was doing."

"Why does Rill treat you so badly?" Luwanna put all the food she had found into Dree's arms.

"I don't know. I saved his life, but not long after that he turned on me."

"You are using the oris root, aren't you?"

Dree was startled. "How can you tell?"

Luwanna looked at him. "You're sluggish, your eye lids are heavy, and you look ill."

"I can't live without the oris root. Rill gets a supply from the Umbinga people when he brings the...the women. He controls my life with it." Dree felt tears fill his eyes.

"You have no life. Rill owns you body and soul." Luwanna said softly. "You have to get yourself off this drug, or you will die." Luwanna looked into the young man's eyes. "Do you understand?" She repeated. "You will die."

Dree nodded.

Chapter Twelve

Tracking

The search party left before first light. In the first few hours of the trip, progress was slow. Everyone had to learn how to manage his animal, and it seemed someone was constantly stopping to adjust something. Abosol couldn't find any tracks at first. So they decided to follow the main path to the Bast territory, and almost immediately, the tracks began to appear.

"I can see three footprints, two small…one large. There is one noogan track. It seems to be following behind. I think Rill is pushing the girls in front of him and leading the animal."

"Well, at least now we have tracks to follow." Coran nodded. "I was getting worried."

"What will we do, if the tracks disappear?" Uri asked.

"Find his home." Chimed in Oden. "I know he is headed for his home."

"How do you know that?" Uri asked.

"It makes sense." Oden answered.

"Ooh… I see." Uri tried to hide the sarcasm in his voice.

They only covered a few miles that day.

The next day they saw more progress. Everyone seemed to fall into a marching mode and the animals began to cooperate.

After crossing the Bast River and traveling until dusk closed in, the group stopped for the second night under the stars. Coran thought it best to camp in this protected area for the night. He chose a spot where there was a large clearing for the animals, and bushes to protect everyone. They could spread out their five bedrolls on the ground to form the shape of a pentagon. Coran started the campfire in the center area so everyone was the same distance away, and received the same amount of heat and light.

Coran and Oden had organized the trip, and everyone complied with the chores allotted to them. Oden was in charge of cooking the evening meal, and preparing the morning hot crost and biscuits. The clean up was Abosol's job, both night and morning. Coran was in charge of the fire. He started one when they stopped for the night and kept it smoldering until dawn. Then got it roaring again in the morning, making sure it was completely dead before they left the area.

Jai was responsible for laying out everyone's personal towels, soap, and other cleansing material every night after dinner. Then before he lay down for the night, he cleaned and packed it all away for the next night.

Uri's job was tending the noogans. He removed their burden of supplies every night, brushed, and wiped them down. Then he tied them to a rope that stretched across the clearing. This way they could move about, but not wander off. He fed them twice a day and made sure they had water to drink during the daily trek. He enjoyed his duties and began to notice each animal had its own personality and quirks. At first, he only named his noogan, Igi. However, before they traveled very far in the journey, each one had its own name. Wiggle was Coran's, and Tommi belonged to Oden. Gala and Jela were the two females, they were Abosol's and Jai's. The one for Bo was the most obstinate. Uri named him Pushi because it seemed he had to push the animal constantly to keep him moving.

Uri came back from tending to the noogans, and sat by the fire ready to consume his dinner. Oden looked around, and seeing everyone assembled, he began to serve. After they ate and cleaned up, they bedded down. The fire flickered brightly, and sparked whenever a bug got too close. Uri was lulled to sleep by the rhythm of the flames as they leapt into the air.

It was late into the night. Something woke Uri. He listened to the restless rustling and snorting of the noogans. Since the animals were his duty, he got up and went to check on them without waking the others. Something he would never do again.

The single moon made the vegetation stand out, but not light the area. He easily made his way to where he had tied the noogans on the ropes. The first warning was he noticed their eyes shone brightly with fear. They were moving against each other chaotically. Then Uri saw it. A large getiru. The eyes were dots of angry flames. It crouched down and began to move toward him, low and menacing. The grotesque face twitched, and pulled back its lips exposing huge, sharp, fangs. Uri felt the hairs all over his body stand straight up. Terror gripped his heart and it seemed to stop. He knew not to run, but he had to do something. In a split second, Uri gulped in a deep breath, and raised his arms, trying to appear as large as possible. Then he screamed, loud and long, jumping up and down. The getiru was startled and stopped.

From behind Uri came more screams, hollers, and someone was banging on a pot. Uri dare not look, but keep his eyes on the beast. The getiru, frightened by all the people and commotion, put his tail between his legs and turned. Running, he vanished into the brush and into the night.

"You sure got here quick." Uri said breathless.

"That scream made us move. It was bone chilling." Coran said.

"I was awake and saw you shuffle over to the animals." Oden said. "I thought something might happen so I got up and grabbed a stick. Then you screamed. Never wander off in the dark," he warned.

Uri hated to admit that Oden was right. His heart still pounded in his chest and made him weak. So, without another word, he returned to the camp and lay back down on his mat. One by one, his companions did the same. However, not one eye closed for the rest of the night.

Oden and Coran left the group to get Bo before the sun rose and illuminated the morning sky. They brought him back just as everyone began to stir. Informed of the situation, he was eager to assist.

However, it wouldn't be for the whole trip. Bo had promised to travel to the Mountain People and visit with his brother Kee, who was living with them. Kee could never come home. Because of his refusal to be the Bast head priest's apprentice, he was declared an Undesirable. Bo tried to visit him as often as possible, and bring him news of their parents and other members of the family. No one knew where Kee was, and their father had declared Kee dead to them.

Uri was glad Bo had agreed to join them, even if for only a short time. Now he might have help with the animals.

Abosol calculated the direction Rill was taking, so they picked up where they left off and moving down the back trails, traveled southwest, passed the Bast village that was located further north of them. Uri noted landmarks along the way, in case they needed to come back this same way.

It was a grueling trek, through the bush and climbing over hills strewn with large rocks. In the afternoon, a clearing came into view in front of them. As they moved closer, Uri notice a hut appeared in the center. The surrounding area was littered with trash.

They continued to approach with caution. Uri looked to see if any animals were in the area. He had a feeling, a suspicion that someone was inside. Abosol crept forward, a knife poised in his hand. Coran and Jai followed behind him. Uri went around, behind the hut with Oden and Bo. They all arrived at the front together. Abosol pushed on the door and it opened easily. Uri saw a figure on the bed. The darkness did not divulge any details, but he knew it was not Rill.

Coran, Bo, Uri, and Oden walked in, moving toward the bed. Leaving Abosol and Jai outside to watch. A small figure, bathed in sweat writhed in obvious pain. Coran knelt beside the boy. He checked his pulse and said, "No fever. I think he is reacting to something he ingested."

"He might know where Rill and the girls are." Oden said, "Can you wake him?"

"Not in this state of delirium. Bo, gather some leaves from the fineal plant."

"The one with feathery leaves?" Bo asked.

"Yes. It smells bad when picked. Get as much as you can carry." Coran yelled after him.

"I'll help." Jai offered and ran after Bo.

"Uri, start a fire and heat some water."

Uri hurried out to complete his task. When he returned inside the hut, he saw Coran wiping Dree's face with a cool, damp cloth. The boy moaned and flailed about.

Several minutes passed before Bo and Jai returned carrying a large bundle of the leaves.

Uri watched as Coran took the leaves and smashed them into the boiling water. Soon the leaves shrank to limp, black threads, and the sweetness aroma drifted up from the liquid.

"It went in stinky and now it really smells good." Uri observed.

"Strange, isn't it?" Coran looked up with a thin smile on his face. "This is powerful, and should bring him around."

Together they lifted Dree to a sitting position and poured as much of the sweet, dark liquid down his throat as they could.

"In about an hour he should be up and able to talk to us. Meanwhile," Coran directed, "Uri unpack the animals and Oden, please prepare our evening meal." Then Coran looked around the hut. "Jai, would you clean up this mess?"

"Sure." Jai replied cheerfully.

Uri followed Coran out of the hut, and began his chores with the noogans. As he finished, savory odors drifted around the area of the hut. Uri felt his stomach react. He was very hungry.

Chapter Thirteen
Arrival

Luwanna stopped her forward movement. The wind had blown constantly all day. It was cold and wet. This was deep into the third day of their travels. Her feet were numb, and would not take that next step.

"Hey!" Rill cried. "Keep up with us."

"I can't, I am exhausted." Luwanna breathed heavily, watching her breath rise in a fog above her. "I'm so cold. Please let me rest."

The noogans, feet buried in those white, frozen flakes, shuddered and emitted a noise to let everyone know how uncomfortable they were. Luwanna understood their complaint, because she also felt the pain those white flakes caused.

"I suppose if I don't stop you'll die, and you are no good to me dead." Rill walked back to her. "Come, get on my noogan." He grabbed her by the arm and dragged her over to his animal. She felt so weak, he had to pick her up, and place her on the back of the large muscular animal.

He nudged the animal forward and they made their bumpy way down the rocky road to the meadow below. The air warmed up, and Luwanna began to feel better. Aleeta began to stir and looked back at her, trying to offer a smile. Luwanna watched the surroundings intently, impressing each feature on her brain. She knew if she could get free, she could make her way back. She kept her eye on Aleeta. Rill covered her with blankets all through the journey. Even so, Luwanna could tell he realized he was pushing her to the brink of exhaustion.

With a quick pace, they were through the meadow and came upon cliffs on either side of the trail. The landscape began to transform. Luwanna watched in amazement as water accumulated into streams, widening as they plunged over the cliffs, and converted into high waterfalls. Vegetation bloomed and grew high into lush forests. While they followed the circling trail downward, flowers appeared in ever-increasing number. Near the bottom of the waterfalls the water pooled into blue lakes, some large, some small. Luwanna saw them everywhere. The air changed, warm and humid. Aleeta looked at Luwanna and shook her head in wonder at the beauty of this place. It was as if they traveled to a different world. Luwanna looked behind them and saw the mountains they rode through, looming high into the clouds. The tops were white with accumulated frozen flakes that rained down on them the day earlier. Now, before them, past the meadow, stood a new set of cliffs rising high into the sky.

They quickly came upon a structure built with logs and a thatched roof. It was open on all four sides and two men leaned over the rail, watching as they approached.

Rill called out. "Passing through with two women for Tri-Po." They seemed to know Rill and they waved him over. He left Luwanna and Aleeta with the noogans, and went over to chat with the men. They passed something between them and laughed heartily at what Rill said.

In a few moments he was back, grabbed the rope leading the animals and the girls past the outpost and into the trees ahead.

Luwanna and Aleeta heard the village before they saw it, a collection of busy voices and traffic. The trail converted from dirt to cobblestones and ahead in the street and side areas, people moved about in great numbers. Still the cliffs loomed in on both sides. Luwanna looked up into openings. The girls locked glances, and Luwanna realized these were dwellings, and they lined the sides of the cliffs, some four stories high.

Trees and huge flowers grew by the front near the street. They softened the starkness of the cliff dwelling. Some plants were living in clay pots, placed on window shelves. Between a few of the dwellings, trickling water that fell from great heights, and entered pools etched in open areas. It was an amazing sight, beautiful and peaceful.

There was much detail around the windows, doors, and columns. Bright colors painted on the front indicated these were individual homes. They were so large, Luwanna figured extended families could live together in one. Grandparents, aunts, uncles, all the children, and so on. She vaguely remembered that Uri talked about a place where he saw dwellings similar to these. Were these related in some way? However, the thought was fleeting and she concentrated on the scene unfolding in front of her.

They continued down the street and passed into the business area. Luwanna noticed many wagons drawn down the streets by noogans. They passed open shops on both sides of the street, selling all kinds of merchandise and food. Odors drifted over the entire area, and Luwanna drew in a deep breath, enjoying the smells. She couldn't identify the variety of foods, but it all smelled good. She realized how hungry she was, and her mouth began to water.

People bustled back and forth amid the open market stalls. The venders called out to them, some arguing, and haggling over the prices. Mostly men walked around. Different ages, different dress, but there were very few women.

Young women carried baskets filled with a variety of purchases. They traveled back and forth, some coming to the market place, and some going back to the different homes. They never looked up, not even to watch her pass by. Their eyes stayed on the ground. Silence accompanied them while singularly going about their duties. They dressed in simple white dresses tied at the waist and sandals on their feet. These were not Umbingas. They were young women and girls from different tribes.

She noticed Rill watching her observe the women, and heard him snicker. Her blood ran cold in her veins. What was their fate to be?

Then as they came to the heart of the city, in the middle of the street, stood a large structure surrounded by decking. Rill stopped and walked up to it. A man adorned with bright colored robes and a shimmering hat appeared at the doorway of the structure. With his back stiff and his head tilted up in a regal manner, he approached Rill.

"What have you brought us?" He asked. Luwanna understood the language even with the thick accent. He looked like a Pinola, with brown hair and dark eyes. Of course it couldn't be. She judged by the worn streets and amount of buildings; these people had been here a long time.

Rill answered. "Honorable Tri-Po, I have brought you two more women."

Tri-Po sniffed. "You promised three. Why are you coming here short handed... again?"

"Please, it is getting very difficult to capture women. All the tribes are on alert." Rill bowed. "Give me more time."

"You have no more time. You must pay your debt. No more osis root until you pay your debt." Tri-Po wrapped his robe around him, retreating to the doorway of the structure. "Bring the women to the ready room."

Suddenly men with long spears appeared from the sides and took hold of Luwanna, lifting her off the noogan. They did the same to Aleeta, marched them around to the side doors, leaving Rill behind.

Chapter Fourteen
Placement

Pushed down the darkened hallway, they entered a room lit by bright torches. In front of them was a pool with very blue water, and clothing laid on large high-backed chairs. The ceiling was far above them, and adorned with pieces of shining jewels. Everything here seemed built in a grand scale.

The men left and immediately two women appeared from behind a wooden screen. Luwanna couldn't help notice the screen was painted with a beautiful scene of colorful large birds. It was obvious there was great artistry in the community.

Immediately her attention came back to the women as they pointed to the pool of water. "Take off your dirty clothing and wash in the water." One commanded.

Aleeta began to cry as she removed her once, beautiful dress she wore to the betrothal ceremony.

"Hush, sweetie." Luwanna whispered. "You will get a new wedding dress very soon."

Aleeta just shook her head as the tears dropped from her cheeks.

The water was warm and soothing. It felt good to be clean again. Once bathed, the girls put on the clothes that laid on the chairs. The rough dress was long, but nicely fashioned. The sandals fit well. Also provided was a warm woven coat that Aleeta and Luwanna picked up, but did not wear.

"Come this way." The women ordered.

The girls followed them into a larger room where two men sat at polished desks, writing in a thick ledger. Large, tall windows lined two sides of the room from which Luwanna felt, a cooling breeze.

"Stand in front of us." The man on the left said. He motioned at the two other women. "You are excused." and they scurried away.

"I will ask you a question and you answer quickly."

Luwanna looked at Aleeta.

"Both of you look only at me." He commanded loudly.

The questioning went on and on. "What is your name... what tribe are you from...how tall are you, short, medium or tall ...do you have younger brothers or sisters...can you cook?" When he asked if either one received a serious injury, Luwanna kept the attack of the Getiru to herself. Then they did some physical agility exercises. Luwanna passed easily, but Aleeta was much weaker and did not complete most of them. Luwanna tried hard to understand what these men were looking for, and why all the questions, but she couldn't fathom what was going on.

Finally, the men were done and told them to sit down in the chairs provided. The man on the right rang a loud bell and two women, dressed as the others were, in long dresses and sandals, rushed in from the side doors. They held their hands together and bowed before the men.

"The one called Aleeta, present her to Ky-Jo."

"No!"Aleeta cried. "Let me stay with Luwanna...please."

Her cries and tears did no good. She was lead away, out of Luwanna's sight.

Luwanna fell on the ground, sobbing. "Oh Lord, my Creator, protect her. Stay by her side. Allow no harm come to her. May our salvation from these people be swift."

Luwanna found herself being led out into the sunlight by a young woman. The young woman led her down the street into the outskirts of the city. The cliffs melted away to be replaced by endless fields of growing vegetables and greens. Trees, yielding different fruits grew in large areas, row after row.

"What is all this?" Luwanna asked.

"We are headed into our fields. Growing here are vegetables, roots, trees with fruit. The growing season lasts a long time. Several months from now, it will grow cold and stop raining. Then workers are sent to the market booths, or assigned to assist in planting of new crops. There are men who come and till the ground, cut branches off the fruit trees. Things that women can't do."

"Are we just to work and that is all? Can we have our own time to visit friends or take walks, enjoy other things in life?" Luwanna pressed on.

"Not really. We are slaves and have very little time for ourselves."

Luwanna shuddered.

"Does it rain much?" She continued with questions.

"Usually a little every day. It is a warm rain and no one stops working. We dry off soon after it stops. The weather here is quite pleasant. The cold season only lasts a short time, about three or four cycles of our moons. Then a strong wind blows often and it is unpleasant. It gets dark early in the afternoon and lasts into the morning, but we have a nice fire in the huts to keep us warm at night."

After walking for a long time, they came to a clearing where a multitude of huts stood. The woman called Tinra pointed to a large hut in front of her. "It will be fine." She said softy to Luwanna.

This was the first sign of compassion she had seen for days. "Vorma, the mistress of this group is good and fair." She motioned for Luwanna to enter the darkened hut. In the doorway beside a bed stood a tall woman. *Vorma, Mountain People,* Luwanna thought. The name and the height of this woman caused her to remember back when she and Uri were led to these people by Bo.

"What is your name?" The woman, Volma asked.

"Luwanna."

"Luwanna, you will work in the fields because you are young and strong. This is a ten-hour day shift. You will receive three meals a day. If you complain, one meal will be taken away for two days."

Luwanna wanted to find out about this woman. "Vorma, how long have you been doing this?" she asked.

"This is yours." Ignoring the question, she pointed to the bed they were standing by.

It was clean and came with a pillow and a blanket. "There is a table next to it for your use."

'Would you like to go home?" Luwanna continued, watching for any sign of emotion.

Vorma blinked. "The day starts at daybreak and everyone is in bed one hour after sunset."

Luwanna wondered when this woman had been taken to be a slave "Do you know where my friend is, or where they took her?" Luwanna asked.

"If you continue this questioning we will not get off to a very friendly start." Vorma said sternly.

"Okay, fine." Luwanna sighed. "Is there water available? I'm thirsty."

"There is always water in the back on the tables."

Luwanna got a drink, looking around she noticed Tinra was gone. Then she returned to her bed. She bounced up and down on it. "Seems comfortable enough, and it is clean."

"You will keep it that way." The gruff answer came from behind.

Luwanna turned and stared into the eyes of a tall man. He handed Vorma a book and grinned at Luwanna as he left.

"Who is that?"

"Our supervisor. His name is Py-Sho. He only comes to receive the reports once a week. The reports are how all of you behave." Vorma stared hard at Luwanna. "It pays to be quiet and do your job."

"I miss my family and friends." Luwanna lowered her eyes and continued. "I imagine it doesn't get any easier... does it?" She looked up, directly into Vorma's brown eyes.

She wanted this woman to know she would not give in or give up.

Chapter Fifteen
Dree

Dree realized he was sitting on the edge of his bed. He was amazed at the intense pain in his head, and it took both his hands to hold his head upright. It felt twice as large as it actually was. It would be helpful if his hands would shake at the same rate of speed as his head. Another agony began between the shoulder blades, and followed his spine down to the lumbar area. Everything quivered in torment since he stopped using the oris root.

How many days? He wasn't sure. His stomach lurched, but nothing was left. At least he could sit up without the room turning upside down, and he hoped it was a sign that the worst was over. He had been using the oris root for three years, and now realized it had left him without any human feelings or thoughts. Time continued in a foggy, dream-like state. He didn't know, or care, if it was day or night. He couldn't remember the last time he ate any food.

When Dree first met Rill, he gave him some of the root for his headaches and it worked. However, Rill became more cruel and devious. He reacted differently to the root than Dree. While it slowly sapped all interest and motivation from Dree, it drove Rill to obsess over things, like capturing all those young women. Sure, that gave the both of them access to the root, but Dree knew he could probably get it without selling women to the Umbinga's chieftain.

He was embarrassed When Rill came back with the two women, and made fun of him. The one called Luwanna spoke to him, and told him to get away from Rill. She encouraged him to live life the way it was supposed to be lived, and warned him if he did not stop taking the root he would die. Dree had never thought of that before.

Since meeting Luwanna, he regained the determination to live. No longer did he want to exist in a fog, and being continually tortured by Rill. He had enough of that treatment. He wanted more than only existing. Dree was sure he wanted to live again, and not die. However, he had no idea he would be so sick. He saturated his mind with the oris root for years, and the sudden deprivation of it almost shut down his bodily functions. At one point, he thought he could feel his heart stop as he floated around the room. Then he fell into a deep unconscious state. Dree vaguely remembered having his face wiped down with a cool towel. Was that part of the hallucinations? No. He heard voices outside the hut. They got louder and as the door opened, Dree looked into the faces of three men.

xxx

Uri, Oden, and Coran went into the hut to see how the boy was doing. Coran had given him a mild drink made from those leaves to calm his body. If he was coherent, he might be able to tell them something about where Rill went.

"Look, he is back among the living." Oden said.

Coran went to the boy's side, felt his pulse, and looked into his eyes. "Do you know what happened to you? Were you sick or did Rill do something to you?"

Dree shook his head. "Rill didn't do anything to me. I did it to myself."

Uri looked at this young boy called Dree. He had dark circles under his eyes, bones shown through his translucent grey skin, and the hair on his head was thin and sparse. He looked like death.

"I have been taking oris root for years." Dree struggled to stand. Unable, he sat back down. "I stopped using it a few days ago and now I am suffering the effects."

"What is that... oris root?" Uri asked

"It is something at first makes you feel good, relaxed, you think you are superior, and more powerful than anyone. It is a root from the Umbinga Tribe. Cut up into pieces it is chewed, and eaten."

"Is Rill using it?" Uri asked.

"Yes, that is how the Umbinga Tribe pay him for the young women he brings them."

Coran put his hands on Dree's shoulders. "Did Rill come here with two women?"

"Yes."

"How long ago did he leave and where was he going?"

"I have no sense of time." Dree groaned. "Please let me rest for a while."

Coran sighed, "Okay we will go and have our meal."

The three of them left the hut and joined with the others around the campfire.

After they all finished their meal, Coran carried a bowl of broth into the hut for Dree. Several moments passed before he came back to wave for everyone to come in. Uri rushed to get ahead of Oden and stood at the end of Dree's bed.

The boy was sitting up sipping on the broth.

"Can you tell us where Rill went with the two women?" Coran began.

"Yes, to the south. There is a tribe far to the south. He brings women there, and he always takes the same route." Dree answered.

"Always? Does he do that often?"

"We have taken young women, even girls to the Umbinga tribe several times."

"Explain." Oden stated flatly.

"They ask him for two or three new females for slaves. Somehow, he captures what he needs, brings them here, and prepares them for the hard journey. He starts out with the noogans and travels south, then east. He follows a trail, so that is not the hard part. When the trail reaches the White Mountains, the trail begins to climb, and gets colder. Sometimes tiny pieces of white things fall soft and quiet to the ground. They cover everything."

"Do these white things do any damage?" Uri asked.

"No, but it is very cold. If you keep on the trail it takes several days to get through to the valley, but we found a way that will take you through the mountains in just a day." Dree continued.

Uri whispered to Jai. "How do we know he is telling the truth?"

Jai shook his head.

"How many animals does Rill take?" Coran continued with the questioning.

"It depends. This time he had two and I think he took them both." Dree said. "If you follow him, you will need warm clothing and boots."

"Are there any left here?" Coran asked.

"Maybe, in the cupboard." Dree pointed to the far wall.

Uri opened the cupboard door, and looked into the darkness. "Actually there are two large coats here and a pair of boots."

"Hmm…" Coran ran his hand over his face. "Bo, can you go to the Bast people and barter for three more coats? I know they have them."

"Sure, I will have to make up a story why I need them."

"Tell them you are selling them to some of your friends. That is not a lie." Coran said. "As far the boots go, we have a sample here of how they are made. We will have to make our own."

Coran turned to Oden. His face suddenly looked sad. "You must slaughter one of the noogans. We need the hide and the meat for our journey."

Uri's heart leapt into his throat. No, not one of his friends. Which one would Oden kill? Probably his favorite. He followed Oden out the door, hoping to influence his choice of which animal.

Chapter Sixteen
A Sacrifice

Running to catch up with Oden, Uri grabbed his arm. 'Which one are you going to kill?"

"The largest would be a good choice."

"That would be Igi, he's mine."

"So, he eats more and takes up more room on the narrow trails." Oden reasoned.

Uri knew it made sense to use the largest for the skins, but he could not allow Igi be killed. "What about Pushi? He is almost as big and he causes the most trouble."

"Are you pleading for your noogan?" Oden smiled.

"Yes." Uri admitted.

"Well, come along. Let's compare them."

Uri followed Oden into the pen of the animals. It was hard to keep tears from clouding his eyes. Oden went from one animal to the other. He checked their feet, mouth, and felt their legs and stomach. Finally, he turned and looked back at Uri, allowing that jeering smile grow on his face.

"Well?" Uri began to tremble.

"You're in luck, my friend. Jela has bad legs. She will not make the long trip and will possibly die along the way. She is chosen, and she is a good size animal."

Uri was unable to speak. He just nodded and rushed back to the hut before Oden began to perform the unspeakable task.

Dusk was descending as Oden opened the door to the hut. All eyes turned to him as he entered.

"It is done. I skinned her, then hung the carcass to drain overnight. I strung it high in the trees so any getiru that wanders around cannot reach it. There will be a lot of meat for us, also a large amount of fat. I will pack that away in a special sack. It will come in handy for cooking and if we need to rub on things to make them slippery. I need to use some in making the boots, to rub in the skins and soften them."

"Do you have any idea how to construct the boots?" Coran asked.

"I thought of a way, however it will take a couple of days to prepare the fur and the hide for that." Oden looked at the sober faces. "It was only a pack animal. Don't take it so hard."

Coran moved first. "You did a good job. We all appreciate that."

Abosol came forward and shook Oden's hand. "Thank you."

Uri sat on his sleeping mat. He turned away from the rest and put his head in his arms. He needed time to grieve. With his back to everyone, he curled into a tight ball. In his anguish, he longed to hold Luwanna in his arms.

Now the tears came, and he hid his face as it grew wet. Uri wondered if Coran felt as lost without Aleeta as he did without Luwanna. His cousin continued to put on a brave face in front of everyone, but inside Uri knew he must be suffering.

Uri sighed. Now he must clear the grief in his mind and sleep. Tomorrow would be a long, hard day.

xxx

The next two days passed in a flurry of preparations. Everyone had a job to do preparing for traveling into an unknown territory with unfamiliar weather and unfamiliar features.

Bo stayed long enough to help prepare the bread, gather fruit, and add his knowledge of making dried meat from the great slabs that came off the noogan. Uri and Jai worked with Bo as he sliced long, thin pieces of meat from the carcass.

"You two start a large smoking fire. Let it grow and heat up. Place a lot of vegetation on it so it will smoke. Then, Abosol will cover the smoky fire with a large hide."

Uri and Jai carried out these instructions and talked back and forth.

"You had better use Bo's noogan now that yours was sacrificed." Uri suggested.

"I assumed that was the plan." Jai shook his head. "Jela was a good old girl. I will miss her."

Uri nodded in silence.

"Animals are for our use." Jai continued. "Watching Goth with the animals he raises on his farm, I learned to view them in the way our Creator intended."

"I suppose I never should have named them. It is easier to become attached." Uri said.

"You have a tender heart, my friend." Jai smiled as he began to hang the pieces of meat on long wooden poles over the hot smoke. Crushed hard, red, berries gathered from nearby bushes, seasoned the meat, and it soon an enticing aroma filled the air.

"I have to say, she smells wonderful." Uri grinned.

In the last two days, Uri felt like an eternity had passed. He yearned to get started, because he knew that wherever Luwanna and Aleeta might be, they were frightened and in danger, waiting to be rescued. He closed his eyes, blotting out the image of Rill prancing around the girls, taunting them. Uri shook with impatience. Meanwhile, a great admiration for Coran grew in Uri's heart. His cousin had the ability to put his emotions aside, and concentrate on the task before him. Coran's many years studying and practicing his priestly duties resulted in a fine-tuned mind. Perhaps there might come a time when Uri could master the patience, courage, and deep abiding faith Coran demonstrated.

The sun rose brightly on the day of departure. They gathered to eat what they all knew would be their last decent meal for a long time. Uri walked around each noogan making sure the straps were not too tight, and each load was balanced correctly. He fed and watered the animals, affectionately rubbing and patting them. He hurried to finish, then headed to the circle the men forming in front of Rill's hut. There was Jai, Coran, Abosol, Oden, Dree, and Uri.

Abosol asked Dree to draw a map on the ground of the route they would take. Everyone squatted and watched intently.

"When you leave here you will follow the trail where the Bast River meets the sea. You will be traveling south through the brush, and you will come to a trail that breaks off and heads east. In a while, the trail begins to climb up into a rocky

84

landscape. As I said before, the higher you go the colder it gets. You will come to an area on the trail where tall trees begin to grow. They are very old and large at the base. After you pass the first few trees, they thin out. Soon you will see a grove of them on your left. You can't miss them. It would seem that the way to go is straight ahead into the mountains. Instead, go to your left, east, through the trees and keep climbing a natural trail through the rocks. You will come to a lone tree on your left. Stay away from that tree. Mysterious things happen there. It is a place where evil spirits live."

Uri and the others looked at each other, but no one said anything to contradict Dree about the Basts belief in evil spirits.

Dree continued. "Leave the trail and climb down into the canyon behind the tree. That is the short cut. A large meadow lies below. Be careful as you make your way down through the rocks to that meadow. There the rocks are loose, and if it has been raining they can slide down the side of the mountains in roaring, huge amounts."

Uri watched Dree looking from face to face.

"It can be very dangerous." Dree warned. "From there you will need to find tracks. That is the only way you can follow where they have traveled."

"How many days are you talking about?" Coran asked.

Dree shrugged. "Only a couple. It takes time to climb all the way through the mountains, but after you pass through the trees and descend the rock sliding area, you can make good time through the meadow."

"Are there no paths?" Coran asked.

"No, it is all grassland, a large meadow. When you have traveled through the meadow in the correct direction, you will come across a path that will lead you to the city of the Umbingas." Dree sat down. "I wish I could come with you, but I'm still not well."

"It might be a good idea for you to go home to your parents. They can assist you in healing." Oden suggested.

"I agree, and I will do that in a couple of days when I feel stronger." Dree replied.

"I also suggest you seek out Bo and ask him about evil spirits, and have him tell you about the one, Holy Spirit." Coran said softly. "It will take away that that cold empty spot inside of you that you tried to fill with the oris root."

"Is the Umbinga Tribe friendly?" Oden asked, changing the subject back to the task. "When we enter the city, will they receive us warmly or what?"

"They will be cautious, but they are not warlike. In fact, they can be very hospitable. However, when they find out what you are after, you will not be welcomed."

"We will have to be diplomatic." Jai said.

"We can't let them know we are after the girls." Uri warned.

"Well, we can form our plans later." Coran said. "Now it is time to leave."

Uri looked to the southwest, the area the trek would begin from in just a few minutes from now. The emotion of anxiety mixed with a sense of urgency. However, first Coran lifted his hands to offer a prayer to The Creator of All for safe passage and for the protection of the girls. Uri lifted his hands, as he implored the Creator in his own way.

Chapter Seventeen
Among the Umbingas

Luwanna looked down at the steaming bowl of mush. She wasn't used to this bland diet, but ate it in order to fill her belly. Mush made up almost seventy percent of her diet since she arrived in the Umbinga village. Luwanna had found out Aleeta went in a different section to work inside with the Umbinga women and children, but because Luwanna was strong and sturdy, she went to work in the fields surrounding the village.

Asking around, Luwanna learned from another other slave girl that Aleeta went to serve a village official's wife. Thankfully, she hadn't seen Rill since they arrived. If she knew where he was in the village, she would be tempted to sneak up on him and kill him with her bare hands.

The trek over the cold and icy mountains almost proved too much for Aleeta. If Luwanna had not been along, Aleeta would have died, she was sure of that. She gave praise to the Creator that He chose to send her along to protect and care for Aleeta. Soon Uri and the others would come and rescue them. She offered that prayer everyday.

After breakfast, the slaves went to the assigned areas to work for ten hours every day. The noon meal, served in the fields, consisted of cold, leftover mush and a cup of Kavac milk. Those furry, little animals seemed to thrive everywhere. In the evening, the Umbingas gave all the exterior slaves a piece of fruit and a biscuit with bits of colored food in it with their allotment of mush. Luwanna wondered what those colored bits of food were. Maybe scraps of vegetables, or leftover dried meat. She turned and scratched another line in the wooden post by her assigned bed. Day number eight. Rescue would be soon now.

As Rill proceded along the trail, Luwanna watched Aleeta drop colored beads from her pocket on the way. Those beads lasted until they got into the valley leading to the village. It was a wonderful idea. She hoped the rescuers would notice the first bunch. Aleeta dropped a large group at the beginning to get their attention. She had smiled at Luwanna and winked.

As she thought about how smart Aleeta was, Luwanna ate the last spoonful of the mush and placed the bowl on the floor next to her bed. Another girl moved beside her.

"My name is Tinra. I know you are Luwanna. Where are you assigned today?" She asked.

Luwanna shrugged her shoulders. "I guess where I was yesterday. Harvesting the greens."

"You know the weather changes here. Even though it is sunny most of the time, it will get very cold in a few months. Even during those months, they have houses where vegetables are grown. Heat from underground is piped into the houses so there will always be greens and vegetables to harvest or plant."

"I guess they will keep us busy." Luwanna turned to the tall girl with brown hair. "I heard that sometimes we go to other places to work in those cold months."

"A few do go away. Sometimes they don't come back. I am not sure if they stay where they had been assigned or what happens to them."

"Tinra, where are you from?"

"I am from the mountain people. So is Vorma, but she has been here longer."

"How long have you been here?" Luwanna continued questioning her.

"I've lost track of the months. It could be years now. I don't know." Her long brown hair fell into her face as she bowed her head.

"Is it possible to visit one of the caretakers?" Luwanna referred to the name given the slaves that cared for the Umbinga women.

"Is there someone you want to visit? They must be a relative in order to get permission. I have a sister there and they allow me to visit her." Tinra said.

"How would they know if she was my sister or not?" Luwanna questioned.

"Oh, they know." The girl shook her head. "Remember when you arrived? How they asked you all those questions? They know if you have a sister here."

Luwanna's face showed her disappointment.

"If you wait for a couple of days, the monthly Gathering of the Faithful will take place and you might be able to find her in the crowds then." Tinra offered hope.

"What is that Gathering for?" Luwanna asked.

"It is a religious gathering. It takes place outside of the village by the god-rock, Bilee. I know you believe in the Creator, I've seen you pray. I too believe." Tinra whispered and grabbed onto Luwanna's hand. "They are idol worshipers, but they leave us to our beliefs. The slaves usually gather in the back of the crowd. However, not all the caregivers are there. If the woman they are caring for is newly birthed, her caretaker must stay with her and can't go to the gathering."

"Why do the women in this tribe need to be waited on? It seems to be an obsession." Luwanna asked.

"All their women are worshiped because new life comes from them. They never work and are fed sweets and fatty meats. They lay around and the slaves wait on them, rub them with oils, and bathe them everyday. Some even ask to be fed." Tinra shook her head. "It's disgusting."

"That is terribly unhealthy." Luwanna observed. "These women must be sickly."

"Yes, and that leads to more care. They get fat and when it is time to have their babies, sometimes they die. Sometimes the babies die too."

"This is stupid." Luwanna grunted.

Tinra looked away from Luwanna's probing eyes. "Sometimes their husbands give them small pieces of the oris root."

"What!" Luwanna was horrified. "I have seen someone very sick because of it."

"Oh, they don't get that much. It keeps the women quiet." Luwanna sighed. "Something needs to be done."

"It is a vicious cycle." Tinra continued. "The more they pamper the women, the sicker they are, and the more deaths. So, the men think they need to give the women more sweets, and less activity."

"If they were given fruits and vegetable with a little exercise they wouldn't need caregivers." Luwanna observed. "Hasn't anyone told these men the facts?"

Tinra laughed. "They don't listen to anyone, especially females."

"When Uri gets here they will."

"Who is Uri?" Tinra asked.

Luwanna just shrugged, realizing she said more than she should have.

She looked around her assigned area, making sure everything was clean and tidy before leaving to begin the days work. This tiny space contained her bed and a table. Next to her sat another bed and table, and so on throughout the hut. Eight slave girls lived here, watched over by Vorma. She was more of a guard than a fellow slave. The huts were so numerous, row after row, it looked like a village within a village.

Luwanna studied as many girls as possible. Mostly they were Bast, and Mountain People, like Vorma and Tinra. She did see a few blonde-haired Dombaras and even several Mudans. Luwanna waited to get alone with them to see who they were, and how they got here.

She worked with these girls side by side with for the last eight days, and observed they were of various ages. They all wore the same expression of fear and hardly spoke to each other. Everyone seemed resigned to this life of hardship. Luwanna decided she would offer kindness and friendship whenever possible. She would represent her Savior in this horrendous environment, and perhaps lighten the burden of the slaves she could reach. However, she felt it would not be wise to talk about the Creator or the Savior outright. She felt the need to be careful.

It was time to leave for the day's labor. They marched out of the hut, and down the well-worn path in single file. In a very short time, they arrived at the fields of various vegetables.

Each woman had her assigned area to pick. Luwanna went to begin where she left off yesterday. Carrying a basket and wearing a bonnet to keep the sun off her face, she settled down to work. Luwanna looked at her hands as she dug in the ground, lifting the green, leafy vegetables into the basket. They had begun to crack and dirt settled in, filling those cracked places as if belonging there. She gritted her teeth. This would not, could not last much longer. There were times when she missed her family and Uri so much, she felt sick to her stomach.

Hours passed and she wiped her forehead, looking down the long rows. All she could see was girl after girl, working as if they had lost all hope for a life. *"If we all stood up,"* she thought, *"and refused to do this… we number more than they do… we could run away. We could rebel and stop this insanity."*

She looked up as the water girl, Keera, offered her a drink. "I have a message for you from Aleeta." The girl whispered and handed her a drink from a cup. Luwanna's back went rigid as she accepted the drink.

"She said she is safe and being well cared for. She has plenty to eat and is doing the best she can. Look for her at the Gathering."

Luwanna handed her the empty cup. "Thank you." She whispered back.

Chapter Eighteen
The Road Ahead

Uri, Coran, Abosol, Jai, and Oden led the noogans along the well-worn trail toward the sea. Their silence told the story of how intense the search had become. Sunshine floated in and out of the trees, making patterns on the hard dirt of the trail. Abosol led the way, watching and marking the tracks in front of him.

He turned to the others. "I can't be sure these are the tracks Rill and the animals made. There are several sets on top of each other."

"It hasn't rained in this area for a few months, so he could have come back and forth here with out water washing away the old ones." Coran said.

"Here the tracks lead off in another direction. Do we follow those or stay with the ones on the path?" Abosol questioned.

"Dree said to stay on the path until the Bast River reaches the sea." Jai said.

Uri added, "I think we should follow Dree's directions."

Silently they all continued down the path. It wasn't long before Abosol shouted.

"Ay… look here."

In the grass, along side of the dirt trail, lay several colored beads.

"These belong to Aleeta. She is showing us the way!" Coran shouted.

Uri marveled at the girl's presence of mind, to think about using the beads from her betrothal party to point the way.

"Keep a watch out for more." Coran said.

Abosol pulled at his noogan, and they began the trek again. This time with a lighter step, knowing they were headed in the right direction.

The sun was high in the blue sky, when the noise of rushing water reached them. Uri pushed through the brush on the side of the trail to reveal the Green Sea below them. A high cliff separated them from the water. To his right he saw the Bast River. It tumbled over the rocky cliff, falling headlong into the sea. A heavy mist rose from the bottom and enshrouded the rocks above, and in the middle was a large, bright arc of color. The view astounded Uri. The rest followed, and they all stood on the edge of the cliff, staring at the scene in front of them.

See how our Lord points the way with beauty and majesty." Coran spoke softly in awe.

That evening they stopped in a clearing, started the night's fire, and Oden began cooking their dinner. Uri unloaded the animals and rubbed them down. He always gained a peace in his soul when he worked with them. They calmed him with their grunting and nudging. He opened the food sacks and gave each of them an allotment of dried greens. There was plenty of grass in the area so he cut back on their dry food, urging them to munch on the grass. Finally finished with his chores, Uri headed back to the comforting glow of the fire.

Coran offered prayer before the evening meal. While they ate, Abosol spoke.

"Do we have any plans for when we reach the Umbinga city?" He looked at Coran. 'What are we going to do?"

"We can't walk right in and demand they give us back our girls." Jai said.

"No, we have to convince them to, or kidnap them back." Coran answered.

"I have an idea." Uri spoke up. He had been thinking about a plan for many nights. "Two or three of us enter the village as visitors. The rest of us scout around in the hills, and learn how the city is laid out."

"You mean go in as spies?" Jai asked.

"Uh... yes I guess so." Uri replied. "It will take time to learn about them and their customs. Where they keep the slaves and what they do with them."

As they silently pondered a plan, the noisy night insects played various tunes. Uri listened for any rustling from the noogans. All was quiet.

Coran broke the silence. "Fine, Abosol and I will enter the city and ask to see the chieftain. We will describe ourselves as travelers, and ask for a place to rest for a few days. Usually people will be hospitable, and offer travelers respite. During that time, we can wander and poke around to learn how they conduct their lives."

"If you act as if their way of life is marvelous to you, flatter them an they will be glad to share details." Oden. "Remember Coran, keep your blonde hair covered. It will immediately give you away as a Dombara."

"We need to find where the girls are," Uri urgently pointed out. "As quickly as possible."

"After the first day we are in the city, we will meet with you, Jai, and Oden in the outskirts."

"We can decide on the point of contact before we split up." Oden added.

They became quiet pondering what lay ahead for them. Uri rolled over and lay on his sleeping pad, looking up into the night sky.

xxx

The morning dawn was cold and clear. As the group moved around, preparing for the day ahead, Uri studied the landscape ahead of them. Mountians loomed high with white, glistening peaks. The trees were a type he had never seen before. Not very tall, but foliage began high toward the top and grew wide and flat. Many birds flew back and forth. Landing on one tree, chirping and calling to others, they flew on to another. The forest seemed alive with movement and noise. Some birds radiated colors, while others were drab and hard to see.

As Uri loaded the noogans, he hummed a tune, soft and calming. The animals swished their ears back and forth, snorting, and touching him with their noses. Their tails flicked at flying insects trying to land for a free ride. Uri looked at the trail ahead. It curved to the left, around a bend and disappeared into the forest. Where were those tall large trees growing in groups or the frozen white flakes Dree spoke of? Perhaps they would appear later today. The air was increasingly colder, and Uri shivered as he put on the heavy coat given to him before they left. He had taken his hair out of it's braid and let it hang over his ears, trying to keep them warm.

By the time they stopped for the first break in the day's travel, the blue sky had given way to menacing clouds, accompanied by a sharp wind. Sitting close to each other, they munched on a simple meal. Uri looked again for those tall, large trees. None had appeared, yet. By the time they were ready to push on, white flakes did begin to fall. Soon the ground was white with them, and Uri was glad for the boots made from the noogan's furry skin.

It was late in the afternoon when they came across the first group of trees Dree described to them, large and tall. Abosol held up his hand for the group to come to a stop. Oden ran ahead and examined the trees. Coran joined him and they spoke with much excitement, while Uri looked ahead to the trail in front of them.

It widened, and headed up into the cold where the clouds drifted overhead. It seemed the way to travel. Even the noogans faced in that direction snorting and stomping their feet.

However, Uri remembered Dree's words. He said it would appear the way to go was straight ahead, but turn onto the rocky trail to the left. That was a shortcut to the Umbinga Tribe.

By now, the colored beads were few and far between. However, Coran managed to see two of them heading left. He shouted and pointed to them. Everyone headed their noogan in that direction and began the trek off the main trail.

Chapter Nineteen
The Royal Residence

Aleeta looked at the plate of food in front of her. The flat, clay plate itself was exquisitely painted. Curly green leaves embracing rose flowers decorated the edges. She admired the artistry. On the plate, lay pieces of fruit and in the middle sat an egg. Not a small Ovi's egg, but a large egg with a brown speckled shell.

Aleeta wondered what Luwanna was eating tonight. Knowing her friend was working in the fields saddened her. She picked up the egg and peeled off the shell. Biting into it, a warm, creamy liquid filled her mouth. The yolk was huge. Immediately guilt flooded her mind. She pushed herself away from the group of slaves she ate with, and walked over to the balcony.

"Aleeta, is there something wrong?" She heard Polder, who was the head of the women attending to the mistress, call her.

"No," she answered, not turning her head. She grabbed the railing and stared into the night in the direction of the fields.

When Aleeta first saw the home of the Chieftain, built into the front of the high cliff, she was so frightened. Inside it had been excavated, and hollowed into spacious rooms. The genius of how they made their homes filled her with awe. Etched into the walls, designs and dancing figures appeared everywhere. The stairs to the upper floors, cut from the rock itself, polished by years of wear, gleamed with hues of colors.

The only light entering the residence came from slanted skylights. She counted six, all draped with a shimmering spun cloth.

Aleeta remembered being ushered up the stairs, and into an outer waiting room. She sat on one of the high pillows covered with a shiny, soft cloth.

A woman appeared. "My name is Polda, maid servant to our mistress, Lai-Po. You will become her 'calmer' which means you will be trained to massage her body with oils." She inspected Aleeta. "Come with me. I will show you your quarters and give you an appropriate robe to wear. Our midday meal will be served in a few minutes. You will meet the women here in this part of the household. Then your training will begin. Polda turned and lifted her head high. "Follow me."

Aleeta obeyed, trembling.

Now she was trembling again, in the cold night air. Her hand holding the railing, white and thin, shook violently as she thought of Luwanna. She felt a warm shawl draped over her shoulders. "Come back in, Aleeta. I know you are worried about your friend."

Aleeta was thankful for her immediate bonding with Polda. "Thank you." she muttered, and went back to sit with the others.

From here, she could see Lai-Po as she lay on her couch. Heavy with child, her fifth, the large body covered the wide bed. Aleeta thought she looked very uncomfortable.

Lai-Po whined incessantly. Never pleased with anything, she complained day and night. Aleeta learned the men of this tribe pampered, and fattened their wives, in order to produce children for them. Aleeta knew this was a horrible misunderstanding and said so every chance she had. She had even asked to speak to the High Chieftain himself to explain. However he had no interest in anything a female had to say. So instead, she encouraged Lai-Po to get up and walk around. "You need to get some exercise, my Lady." She entreated her. But, the woman only moaned and complained that her back hurt. "It will help your back." Aleeta pleaded to no avail.

"Why do you bother?" Polda asked.

"Because it is not right. I care about these women and great harm is happening to them because of inactivity and bad food."

Once the other day, Aleeta offered Lai-Po her fruit, but it created such a tirade, she didn't try again.

Now a slave girl hovered over Lai-Po, feeding her bits of sweets and meats.

"No, no, no." She cried. "I don't want anymore of that lousy food. Rub my feet. Call for Aleeta to come and rub my feet."

Aleeta immediately grabbed a vial of sweet oil and ran to her.

"Yes my Lady." she called. "Here I am."

"Aleeta," the mistress moaned. "You are the only one that listens to me. You are the only one who cares."

"No, my Lady we all care and love you."

Lai-Po sat up on her elbows. "Why are you so kind?"

Aleeta smiled. She knew the Creator had put her in this position for a reason. The Savior spoke of being a servant to all. That was the highest calling. She wanted to follow her Lord's example. He gave this great blessing to her. To serve the most important wife of the tribe to the best of her ability. Lai-Po was about to deliver her fifth child. None of them lived, except for one boy, now seven. Perhaps if she helped Lai Po, this next child would also live.

"My Creator wants all of His children to be kind to each other."

"Oh, your Creator, that's right. Tell me another story of this God."

While Aleeta rubbed and massaged Lai-Po's feet Aleeta thought through the stories in the Great Book.

"There was a man traveling south from a place called Jersum to his home in another great city." She began. "Along the way, robbers attacked him, beating, and stealing everything he had. He lay in the road, left to die. A high priest of that land came across him and seeing him bleeding and unconscious, did not want to spend the time to help. So, he crossed over to the other side, and ignored the unfortunate man. Another man, from his own people did the same. Then a man from a detestable city all of the people in the land considered lowest of the low, came across him. He saw how badly the man was beaten and needed help. It didn't matter who came from where or who was from where. He saw a man that needed help. He took the time to bandage his wounds, put him on his own noogan, and brought the beaten man to a place where he could be cared for. He even gave the owner of the place money to pay for this mans care."

"So this lowly man helped someone who probably would not have helped him." Lai-Po said.

"That is true. Our God tells us to treat everyone as a brother and to love each other no matter who it is."

"I could not do that." The woman said truthfully.

"If you knew my Savior, you could and would want to." Aleeta smiled as she finished the massage. She knew all the others listened to the story. She felt comforted, and the depression she felt earlier left.

Chapter Twenty
The Gathering

At last, the night of The Gathering was here. Before she left the hut, Luwanna combed her hair, pulled it to the side, and tied it with a colored strip of cloth.. Then she slipped on a clean dress. She quickly followed the crowd moving toward the outskirts of town to gather at the god-rock Bilee.

The cliffs that bordered this end of town fanned out on either side. Here and there, outcrops of tall rocks leaped from the valley floor. They followed a stream that wound its way around the trees and rocks until it trailed off to the right. In front of her, looming up in the darkness was a huge outcropping of rocks. One twisted to the left and next to it, torches lined the pathway beside it. Shadows flickering off the front of the huge rock in front, and Luwanna began to make out a face mirrored in the stone. Flowers, and wreaths made from green grasses, adorned the top of the head-like structure. A fire roared in front of the altar.

So, this was the god-rock Bilee. It didn't look like a face cut into the rock. The stone itself undulated into hollows for eyes, a bump for where a nose should be and a long crack for a mouth. At the top of the stone head was a high forehead, slanting backwards. Luwanna was amazed. It was hard for her to believe that these people, with such a developed culture, would worship a hunk of stone.

She hung back with the other slaves and searched each face for Aleeta. The fires grew brighter in the increasing darkness of the night and illuminated all the gatherers.

She turned around and looked at the group coming up behind her. Then she spotted someone waving in her direction. Squinting, she saw it was Tinra and beside her Aleeta. Luwanna pushed her way back through the crowd and reached Aleeta with lightning speed.

"Oh my dear." She hugged Aleeta so tightly she pushed the breath from her. "Are you alright?" She patted Aleeta's shining auburn hair that hung loose around her shoulders.

Aleeta laughed. "Yes, I'm fine. I have been trying to get you transferred to the household, to be with me."

"What is it you do?" Luwanna asked, keeping her voice low.

"I am in the High Chieftain's home, caring for his wife. I massage her with special oils. That is my duty. There are eight of us. One feeds her. Can you believe that? One does her hair every day. Another girl dresses her, and another bathes her. One puts her jewelry on. One even trims her nails and paints them. I am amazed. She is heavy with her fifth child and very fat."

"I heard the men keep the women fed with sweets and fatty meat. That is terrible."

"They believe the reason the women are in poor health is because they bear the children, so they pamper them to an extreme." Aleeta shook her head. "I have been telling the women about the Lord and trying to exercise the mistress more…"

Luwanna interrupted. "You have been talking about Our Creator?"

104

"Yes," Aleeta said, "Every chance I have."

"Do you think that is wise?" Luwanna shook her head. "It will draw unwanted attention to us."

"Isn't telling the Good News to the lost exactly what we are supposed to do?"

"At the right time and to the right people, but I think what you are doing is dangerous." Luwanna replied.

"I believe it is what the Lord wants me to do." Aleeta said flatly.

"Okay, please be careful." Luwanna conceded. "We need to plan how we can be together, alone. My days and evenings are highly guarded. I don't think I dare sneak out in the middle of the night."

Aleeta had been pondering the problem. "I will continue to try and get you transferred to the royal household. I will talk to Polda. She likes me and listens to me when I tell the Mistress Lai-Po stories."

Luwanna shook her head. "It may not be necessary. After all, Coran and Uri should be here any day and…"

"We must be practical. It may not be for a long time. We need to get ourselves in the best position possible. Letting you, work to death in the fields is not acceptable. I will not rest until you are with me."

The drums began to pound by the rock-god and loud singing began. Now they couldn't hear each other talk, so Luwanna grabbed Aleeta's hand and held it tight.

The drums got louder and in the light from the torches and the alter fire, the girls watched the shadows of the writhing dancers. Their silhouetted bodies waved back and forth. Some leapt from the ground with a deafening whoop. Frightened, Luwanna and Aleeta grabbed each other.

From the back of the crowd, Luwanna heard a girl scream. Aleeta heard it too, and they turned to observe a group of men, hooded and, wearing nothing but pants, dragging a young woman to the front where the rock-god, Bilee, and his alter glistened in the moonlight.

"My dear Lord," gasped Aleeta. "What are they doing?"

"I pray it isn't what it looks like." Luwanna whispered. She looked around at the crowd surrounding them. Everyone was straining to see, but silent. The Umbingas, on the other hand let out a loud cheer, approving of the scene playing out before them. As the young woman approached the front, the crowd began to chant. The chant was low and had a malevolent tone. An evil chill invaded Luwanna, and traveled up to the top of her head.

Aleeta squeezed Luwanna's arm. "No, it can't be. Is she going to be a sacrifice?"

Luwanna watched in disbelief as four men lifted the girl high in the air. In front of the fire. Tri-Po rose up from the assemblage. His voice rang loud and clear. "Oh hear us great Bilee, and grant us your mercy. We, your believers, offer you this woman. May you be pleased and satisfied with our offering. May you bless our crops and the fruit of our labors. May you bless our women and grant them health and fruitfulness."

The crowd cheered in approval.

"We mustn't stay and witness this horror." Luwanna looked around for an exit through the crowd. "Come, Aleeta lets get out of here before we see something demonic."

Tri-Po continued. "The fire in your belly will purify this offering and grant her long life and a pure mind as your priestess."

Captured by the moment, Aleeta stared at the ceremony displayed high on the god-rock.

The men who carried her in carved a V on the girl's forehead, and blood instantly covered her face. Then they laid her on the altar, and gathered around her.

"Go." Luwanna grabbed Aleeta's hand. "We must get out of here." she began to feel a wave of nausea overwhelm her. Running clear of the crowd with Aleeta in tow, Luwanna fell to her knees.

"Did you see that?" Aleeta cried. "What will they do to her now?"

As Luwanna fought to overcome the desire to release her dinner from her stomach, a cool hand touched the back of her neck. Looking up she saw Tinra bending over her.

"Are you alright?" she asked Luwanna.

"No, I am not." She stood up and faced Tinra. "What is going on back there?"

"I'm sorry, I didn't know they were going to initiate a girl into the priesthood tonight. It is considered an honor be the god's priestess and live in the temple for the rest of their life. It is usually the girl's choice, but this one put up quite a fuss."

"I thought she was going to be killed." Luwanna breathed deeply, trying to calm herself.

"Oh no! She receives a V on her forehead to identify her as a maiden and then is decorated with tattoos on her arms."

Luwanna turned to Aleeta. "I believe you are right." She closed her eyes and said with great fervor. "We must witness to these people about the saving love of our Creator and Savior. We must be bold and fervent in our testimony."

Chapter Twenty-One
Journey's End

Uri and his friends had come to the place Dree warned them about, the lone tree. The place where he said evil spirits roamed.

Uri detected a strange and quiet heaviness in the area. The hair on his arms stood up. In a circle around the tree, the ground was bare. No grass or brush grew in the area, and birds gave it a wide berth. Black rocks scattered about and Uri noticed several strange piles. Some small like pebbles, and others large as river rocks. Oden walked over, and pushed them with the toe of his boot. A pile of them moved together and others nearby moved on their own toward them. All of the men startled, jumped back, including Oden who ran in the opposite direction, away from the pile of moving rocks.

"What would cause that movement?" Abosol said.

"Wait." Uri walked to the black rocks and picked one up. Several hung on to it. "Look!" He moved the rock over smaller ones and they were attracted to the larger rock. "We talked about this in the Yoka School I went to. My teacher said there was an invisible force that some rocks had. They were attracted to each other and sometimes, other rocks as well." He played around with the rocks, pulling some away and running others across the ground. He looked up and smiled. "No magic or spirits here."

Coran nodded. "Nevertheless, I am uncomfortable here. Let's move on."

They grabbed the reins of the animals and began to pick their way over the sliding, loose stones ahead.

Uri noticed, from the corner of his eye, Oden lingering behind, stuffing some of the stones in his pocket.

"Why would he do that... on the sly?" Uri thought. *"He is sneaky and not to be trusted."* However, at this point, he decided to keep this incident to himself.

The animals had a hard time walking among the sliding rocks, which made the trip down into the meadow below slow and treacherous. They passed through areas of noticeable landsides, where mounds of debris covered the path that otherwise would have been easy to cross. Abosol stopped many times, looking for a safe trail to follow. Uri was grateful for his expertise.

No one spoke while they concentrated on their footing and on their animal's progress. As they neared the bottom of the hills, Jai moved closer to Uri.

"Before we left the trail and came down this way, I noticed the path that seemed correct led up into the mountains covered in white. That would have taken us days to cross."

"I'm glad Dree warned us." Uri replied.

"Have you watched the white flakes when they come down and hit you on the skin?"

"Yes, they turn to water. They seem to be a different form of water, I guess, because of the cold."

"There is so much we don't know about our world." Jai's tone reflected the awe he felt.

"True, however, we seem to be learning more and more." Uri paused. He lifted his head. There was a different smell in the air. Before them, the meadow spread out. It fell gently to the left and a display of colors burst through the grasses, stretching headlong into the hills beyond. There seemed to be new sweetness surrounding them and the breeze blew warmer containing a gentle essence. Trees and plants bore huge leaves. Coran pointed to the far horizen where tall, straight cliffs rose with dozens of waterfalls. "That is our destination."

Uri looked, imagining Luwanna as a captive somewhere in the distance. His heart ached for her.

"It is growing late. I saw a large lake over by that waterfall." Coran said, pointing to the right. "I think it would be a good place to stop for the rest of the day. We can refill our water supply and begin planning how to find an inroad to the city."

They spread out to rest at a grove of trees near the edge of the hills by the lake. Uri fed and watered the animals. They also sensed a more peaceful and safer place, happily munching on the green grass around them.

Strange bird-like animals paddled around by the shore. As he moved closer, they turned and went in the opposite direction. Amused, he threw a pebble in the water, and they fluttered their wings to gain ground between them and the perceived threat.

Uri looked around, enamored by the beauty of this place. In the late afternoon sun, arcs of colors drifted in and out of the mists in the waterfalls. The pooling waters of blue reflected the color of the sky and the bushes surrounding them. Songbirds filled the trees. Their music filtered over the pastoral countryside.

"Don't get too enchanted by this land." Coran said in a low voice next to his ear. "The people who live here steal women for slaves."

"They have picked a very special place to occupy." Uri replied. "I would like to come back here some day."

"Tomorrow we enter their city. Abosol has found footprints in the grass. the blades are bent broken, and the trail is heading toward the area of cliffs. We need to lay our plans." Coran motioned toward the rest of the group circling a small fire in the middle of the camp. "Let us join them."

Uri nodded and sighed deeply. He felt very tired, and wished it were all over.

When everyone settled down, Coran began, "Abosol and I have a few ideas."

Uri noticed that Oden set his mouth in displeasure. Coran noticed it too.

"Sorry Oden that we didn't consult you, however Abosol is our tracker."

"Oh, I have no problem with that." Oden responded quickly.

"We think it would be feasible to go in pretending to be travelers, as we previously said. Go to the head of the tribe and ask for his people's hospitality, maybe trade items, ask directions, and those types of things. If we stay a day or two, we can learn the customs and figure out where the girls are."

"What about the rest of us?" Oden asked impatiently.

"You can try to disguise yourselves as villagers and inconspicuously roam the outskirts of the area. Do not cause any suspicion. Read the lay of the land. In the night go to the camp and wait for Abosol or me to come back with information."

"How will we get the girls back?" Jai asked.

"We need to find out about the Umbinga's society first." Coran said. "Let's take it one step at a time."

"We don't know anything about these people." Abosol cautioned. "Are they warlike, or friendly? Why have they captured women all this time? What do they do with them? First we need to learn their beliefs and the way they live."

"Sounds like a waste of time." Oden grumbled.

"Why don't we find Rill? He can tell us what we want to know." Jai said.

"Do we know Rill is still here?" Uri asked.

"We didn't see him on the trail here. He must be gone." Oden declared.

"We can search for him." Coran replied. "It would be helpful. However, with or without him, we must find the girls."

"Well, I'm not going to bother to look for Rill." Oden shook his head. "He has left."

Coran looked hard at Oden, then continued. "We who are Dombaras need to cover our hair. The blonde color is a dead give away of who we are. That is almost all of us. Oden you don't have to worry. There is a lot of Mudan blood in you, and Abosol is fine."

"We can wrap our heads in cloth." Uri offered.

"Or use hoods." Jai said.

"Does anyone have any other ideas?" Coran asked.

Oden began to open his mouth, and then shut it again.

"Were you going to say something?" Coran asked him.

"What will we use to trade? They might not be willing or eager to give up the girls, unless we offer them something they want," he stated.

"Well, we have the noogans and I brought coins from the Bast tribe." Coran said.

"This whole operation will have to be played one step at a time. If we have to, we can use force." Abosol grimaced.

"If no one has anything else to add, let's get our supper together and settle down for the night. Tomorrow will be a stressful day." Coran stated, looking somberly around the group.

Chapter Twenty-Two
Inside

Coran and Abosol rose just before dawn, and after a small breakfast took two noogans loaded with supplies, they entered the city. Finding the central building where Tri-Po held court, Coran asked for an audience. The leader was pleased to meet travelers who thought his city was important enough to visit and trade goods with. Tri-Po immediately invited Coran and Abosol to his home for refreshments.

Coran and Abosol sat down on pillows, arranged around the mosaic floor of Tri-Po's royal home.

"Thank you for your hospitality." Coran said as he pulled the hood from his robe tighter around his head, hiding his blonde curls.

"How do you come to be here, in our land?" Tri Po asked as a young woman appeared holding a tray with squatty clay cups, filled with a red liquid.

"We are adventurers, traveling all around." Abosol answered.

"How far have you traveled?"

"Many, many days. Our tribe is east past the Dombaras and the Mudans." Abosol seemed to lie easily, without hesitation.

115

"I didn't realize there were tribes that far east. We know of the Bast, Dombaras, and have heard of the Mudans." The eyes of Tri-Po narrowed.

"We are a small tribe." Coran added.

"Yes," Abosol continued. "We are searching around for new people to trade with."

"Oh, what do you have to trade?"

Abosol gasped. "Look, what beautiful girls you have here my lord." Your place here is magnificent. We don't have anything to compare to your city and its splendor."

"Ah yes, the girls." Tri-Po sighed. "Our slaves come from all over. I have some of the loveliest ones in my household to serve me, and my wife."

"How impressive." Coran bowed his head slightly.

"However, one in particular is giving us a problem. She talks incessantly about her God."

Coran's ears perked up. "Really. How disturbing."

"Yes," Tri-Po continued. "She has only been here a week or so, but has all the slaves in an uproar. I am thinking of selling her." He indifferently took a drink from his cup.

"Oh," replied Coran. "We are thinking of buying a young maiden to help us in our travels. Even better, a young man. Do you have any young men for sale?"

"No, we only have females. You would do better with an outside worker. They are much stronger and used to hard work."

"Do you have any newly acquired ones?" Abosol asked.

"Of course, we acquire slaves constantly. What do you have in trade?" Tri-Po asked again, and seemed interested.

116

"Before we talk about that, may we see some of the newer ones you speak of?" Abosol spoke with caution. Praying his pounding heart didn't show through the robe.

"Certainly." Tri-Po said.

"Also, my lord. I would like to see the girl who is causing all this trouble. If you don't mind." Coran said softly, hoping his trembling voice didn't betray him. "If you are intent on selling her, I may be interested."

"Hm… I understand. I will send for her."

Coran and Abosol looked with caution at each other.

"My lord, I would prefer she didn't see us looking her over." Coran smiled humbly at his host. He couldn't believe this was working out so easily.

Tri-Po clapped his hands and his servant bended near to him. The chief whispered something in his ear and watched him scurry away.

"I am sending for the overseer. She will assemble my wife's slaves in the anteroom. We can view them from the balcony that overlooks the bottom floor and I will point her out to you."

xxx

The day had started out quiet enough. The previous night, all the scenes at the Gathering played in Aleeta's mind. She couldn't shake the dark terror that coursed through her mind. It affected her whole being, body, and soul. How could people do such horrible things to one another? She thought of her father and brothers. They also committed hideous crimes. She laid her head in her arms, holding back the tears. The pain in her soul, and aching for Coran overtook her as despair consumed Aleeta's mind.

She felt a hand on her shoulder.

"There seems to be something wrong this morning." The voice of Polda brought her back to her present state.

"I am upset by the ceremony last night," she muttered.

"Ah yes." the woman sat down next to her. "The Umbinga's history is full of violence. Thankfully, it is not as bad as it was in the past. Long ago sacrifices were much bloodier"

Aleeta shuddered, and then looked over at the sleeping Lai-Po. "Their way of confining the wives and mothers of their children is barbaric." She fought back the tears. "Look at her. No wonder the death rate is so high."

"You will have to learn what things you have no control over, and accept them." Polda sighed.

"No, I will not accept them. My Creator did not design for His children to live this way, I will continue to try to bring His saving grace to all whom live in this land, as long as I am here."

As Aleeta spoke, a messenger called to Polda. She went to the curtains that separated Lai-Po bedroom from the rest of her quarters, where a young man conveyed a command from Tri-Po. She turned and clapped her hands. "Listen, all Lai-Po's slaves are required to go and gather in the anteroom, downstairs. I will stay behind with the mistress. Now hurry and go."

Rustling and whispering flowed through the room as all the women gathered and walked in a line down the corridor to the stairs, Aleeta at the back. She did not want to go and looked for a way to escape as they quietly descended to the bottom floor. She slowly lagged further behind. With extreme stealth, she crept behind a column at the bottom of the stairs. Encircling the column, she looked around and up to the balcony on the floor above. A group of men stood with Tri-Po. What was going on?

Her heart stopped and Aleeta lost her breath. The man with the hood over his head glanced toward her. Coran! She would know him anywhere. At last, he was here. Her mind raced. She must be careful. She must not let on that she spotted him. Panic set in. Her heart beating hard in her chest, she scurried to catch up with the others in the anteroom.

The women stood shoulder to shoulder, their hands clasped in front of them, eyes down to the ground. Aleeta moved in next to the end. She straightened her white dress. She put on a new one this morning and belted it at the waist with a braided gold rope. She pulled her hair back and wrapped it with a golden coil after she dressed. The auburn curls spilled out the back of the coil and flowed down her back. She prayed Coran would see she was healthy and safe. He must recognize her. As the seconds ticked by, she heard muffled talking from the balcony. Slowly she lifted her eyes from the floor and straight into Coran's. Their gaze locked for an instant and she lowered them again.

A servant behind pushed her forward, and she overheard the words from Tri-Po.

"That is the one."

She had no idea what that meant. Was he displeased with her? She took good care of his wife. Why did he single her out?

Coran's voice drifted down, loud and clear. "She would do quite nicely."

"*Thank you Lord.*" She prayed. "*He is here safe. Maybe this nightmare will be over soon.*"

Chapter Twenty-Three
Spies into the City

Uri walked with Jai and Oden down the busy street. Jai and Uri wrapped their heads with cloths to hide the blonde hair. They didn't worry about the clothing. It revealed nothing unusual. They attempted to blend in with the rest by looking over the wares and food offered for sale,

Earlier, when they first entered the city, Uri felt rocked to his very foundation when he first saw the homes built into the side of the cliffs. Many mysteries suddenly became clear. This is where those inhabitants of the abandoned cliff-side dwellings ended up. It could not be a coincidence. This culture had many centuries to expand and grow in this area. These people had advanced far beyond the culture that once occupied the cliff-side habitats in Pinola Land.

"Abosol, do you notice the similarity between these dwelling and the ones near the ocean when we saw Zekod and the others?" Uri asked.

"Of course, yes." He answered.

"What are you talking about?" Oden questioned.

Uri ignored him. "They must have been here a long time. The society has grown and flourished here."

"I wonder if there is a face-like rock here," Abosol added.

"I'm sure there is, somewhere."

Oden grew impatient. "Are you going to let me in on what you are talking about?"

"There is a similar area north of Pinola Land. We discovered it when we were looking for Zekod." Uri said, casually.

"That's interesting." Oden was mulling the information over in his mind.

Walking down the main street Uri began to notice the people were looking and watching them. "I think it would be a good idea to travel down the side streets. We are drawing unwanted attention."

"With this many inhabitants you wouldn't think we would be noticed." Oden said.

"We look like we don't belong here." Jai replied.

They cut through the food stalls and meandered down the back streets. Here they saw many buildings with closed doors and small windows. Men walked by who wouldn't make eye contact with them.

"This must be the undesirable part of the community." Jai pointed out.

"Every tribe has some." Uri said, trying not to look at Oden.

The streets had litter and trash scattered about. Men cowered in dark corners in groups of two or three, looking suspiciously at the three newcomers.

In front of them, a door opened and a familiar face walked into the street.

Uri saw him first and gasped. Next, Oden yelped and took off on a frantic run.

Rill looked up. Uri saw astonishment appear on his face, and then he turned to flee from Oden.

Jai and Uri joined in the chase, but Rill quickly ducked into an alley and by the time the three reached it, he had disappeared.

They probed every inch of the alley. No clues presented themselves, but there was one door that he could have gone into.

"Where does this door lead to?" Oden questioned.

"It looks like a storage area." Jai answered, shaking the door and looking up onto the roof.

'We must tell Coran and come back to this area with him." Uri said. "Let's go to the shop Rill came out of. Maybe we can learn more."

They back-tracked to the place where Rill emerged, and opened the door looking into a dark, smelly shop, full of tables where shadowy figures hunched on chairs in groups.

Entering, they sat at the first table near the door. The chairs groaned as they sat. A lantern on the table cast a faint light. As their eyes adjusted to the dark, a large man approached them. His sleeves rolled up and stains covered his shirt.

"Whatcha want." he projected his gravely voice toward them.

"Information about a friend of ours." Oden spoke quickly. "His name is Rill. He is a Dombara."

"A drink here costs one coin, but information is more expensive." He growled back.

Oden reached into his bag of coins, and dropped five on the table. "Will this buy an answer?"

The large man grabbed the coins and slid them into a small bag around his neck.

"Yeh, I know Rill. He comes here most every afternoon. Stays till late in the night. He's is not well liked by us Umbingas. He talks too much and brags about everything."

"Do you know where he goes when he leaves?" Uri asked.

"Nope."

"Thanks, my friend." Oden said and they rose to leave. He dropped two more coins on the table. "These are to buy your silence."

"No problem about that," was the answer.

They emerged into the daylight and fresh air. "Hopefully we can come back tomorrow."

Uri said. "With Coran---and we need to cover the alley where he disappeared."

"Good idea." Jai replied.

"We should get back to the camp. Coran and Abosol will be there after dark." Uri said.

xxx

Nightfall came quickly. Coran and Abosol moved up into the hills and over to where the camp had been set up. Concealed by brush and rocks, it took them awhile to find the right area. Uri sat with Jai and Oden on the ground near the fire. They stood up on guard, as someone approached the area.

"It is Coran with Abosol." He called out.

They all relaxed and greeted each other.

"I have good news!" Coran began. "We found Aleeta."

A joyous cry comes from all of them.

"She is in the house of the leader, Tri-Po. He is anxious to sell her. So, I bought her."

"For how much?" Oden quickly asked.

"Does it matter?" Coran retorted. "I offered two noogans and a bolt of the soft, shiny cloth we brought with us."

"What about Luwanna?" Uri asked.

"We haven't had any word yet. I hope that Aleeta knows. I go to obtain her tomorrow." Coran put his hand on Uri's shoulder. "We will find Luwanna, I promise."

"We also have news." Jai spoke up. "We found Rill."

"Where?" Coran said.

"In town." Uri answered. "He goes to an old shop on the back streets. He should be there tomorrow night.

There was an air of hope in the camp. Oden cooked the evening meal, and they consumed it in a hurry. Uri checked to make sure the animals were safely bedded down for the night. The day's activity, coupled with the emotion, produced sighs and mutterings of exhaustion from everyone except for Uri. He was still wide eyed as they all laid down for a good nights sleep.

Chapter Twenty-Four
Deadly Confrontation

The night dragged on. Uri listened to various sounds of snoring, but he could not relax. The moonlight found a spot between the tree branches and shone directly into his eyes. He continually worried about Luwanna. Could they find her? Did Aleeta know where she was? After a couple of hours, he finally drifted off into a restless doze.

A rustling noise disturbed him. He looked around in the darkness, and to his surprise, Oden was quietly leaving camp. Uri immediately knew where he was headed. He crawled over to Coran, and gently shook him.

"Wake up, Oden just left the camp. I think he is going into town to confront Rill without us."

Coran shook the sleep from his head. "Why would he do that?"

"I'm not sure, but it is very suspicious. We had better follow him."

"I agree." Coran got up and woke Jai and Abosol. Soon together, they walked down the darkened trail into the city.

One moon was setting, but the smaller, Visca, had already topped the trees in the distance. They would have some moonlight to help them follow Oden.

Before too long they arrived at the back streets of the city. Abosol tracked the fresh footprints in the pale moonlight. They knew Oden had entered the shop they visited earlier in the day.

Immediately as they entered the shop, the large man recognized Uri and Jai. He pointed at the back door. "Someone just came in and took Rill. I don't know where they went."

"And we don't care." Someone out of the darkness piped up.

They left and gathered around Abosol as he scrutinized the ground outside of the building.

"This place is full of prints.' He walked around and came back. "There are two sets of prints that lead up into the hills behind us. One of them looks as if they did not want to go. The prints are smeared and appear to be dragging."

They hastened along, following the prints into the nearby hills. Soon they heard loud voices.

"It doesn't matter if it didn't get you the results you wanted. Oden, I helped you and did exactly as you asked." It was Rill's voice.

From out of the darkness, both could be seen, standing on a rise of bare rocks. Coran came up next to Uri's side.

"Oden...What is it you asked Rill to do?" Coran spoke loud and clear.

Oden turned with surprise on his face. Uri could tell he was not happy to see them there.

"This is a private matter. Go away. It is between Rill and me."

"I have a feeling this matter involves us all." Coran commanded. "Tell us Oden."

Rill stood firmly in front of them, "What's the matter Oden? Should I tell them our secret? That you asked me to contact the Bast."

Oden's face grew bright red. "Shut up Rill. You are a liar!"

Rill laughed, touched his lip with his tongue, and doubled up with glee. "Oh yes, who is the liar? Who is the deceiver? You were behind the poisoning plot all along. You and Zekod. However, it didn't go as you expected, did it? The Dombaras did not reject the Bast from the marketplace, did they?" Rill shut his eyes, his hands reached above his head. "This is so great."

Before his horrified eyes, Uri watched Oden remove a knife from its sheath. He yelled a warning as Oden bounded up to Rill and plunged it deep into his chest. Immediately a crimson stain grew on Rill's shirt. His eyes opened wide, and disbelief flushed Rill's face. He fell to his knees on the bare rock in shock. Uri watched the light depart from Rill's eyes, and become vacant. He tipped and fell over sideways, tumbling from the rocks he stood on.

In a flash, Coran and Abosol grabbed Oden and removed the knife from his hand.

"I had to do it," Oden cried, a mask of terror crept over his course features. "He was going to kill all of us."

Coran twisted Oden's arm behind him, bringing his face next to the wide faced Mudan half-breed. "What was he saying about the poisonings, Oden? What was this secret he was talking about?"

"He was lying. He hates me." Oden cried out.

"Did you lead him to the Bast to buy the poisons?" Coran continued questioning Oden.

Uri went over to Rill's still body, and knelt beside it. His head hung in an awkward position. His blank eyes wide open, as was his mouth. Uri put his hand over those staring eyes and closed them. Rill was dead. This time he really was dead.

"You don't understand," Oden began to whimper. "It was my opportunity to get even with the Bast for ruining my life. If the Dombaras found out the Bast were giving the Pinolas poisons, they would refuse to allow them at the market anymore. That would ruin the Bast culture."

"But it didn't work out that way, did it." Uri left Rill's body and approached Oden. He wanted to grab Oden by the neck and squeeze until his eyes popped. All the doubts and suspicions he carried with him for months hit the surface of Uri's mind. Rill was not Uri's friend in any sense of the term; however, he didn't deserve to die in that tragic manner. As he approached Oden it became clear, and the truth washed over him like ocean waves. "That's why you killed Zekod. You were afraid he might have given you away."

"I saved your life." Oden cried.

Coran shook his head in disbelief. "You pretended to be a believer. You pretended to be a faithful Dombara, but you are worse than the pagans that live around us."

Oden looked horrified. "No, I am a believer. However, I have a right to avenge my father's death. Those people, the Bast, they ruined my life. They took away my identity."

"No, you do not have a right for revenge. Vengeance belongs to the Lord." Coran stood straight. "What shall we do with you?"

Oden jutted forth his chin in an attempt to justify himself. "You should be grateful. Rill was an evil man."

"You are just as evil." Coran said. "You cannot be allowed to go free. You have murdered a person."

Jai went to grab his hands, but Oden twisted away. From within his coat came another knife and he wielded it expertly.

"Get away from me. I will kill everyone." Oden said with determination. Fire and hostility flowed from his narrowing eyes. His face twisted with hate until Uri did not recognize him anymore.

Oden backed up while they all watched. When he reached the edge of the trees, he turned and ran, disappearing quickly. Uri leapt forward to follow, but Coran restrained him. "No, don't follow. Besides, where can he go? We'll attend to him later. Our most important mission is the girls."

Uri dropped his arms to his side. He had known there was something very wrong with Oden, but this revelation was a surprise. Stunned by the evenings events, they slowly walked over to Rill's body.

"Shall we bury him here?" Jai asked.

"Here is as good as anywhere." Coran said.

With great somberness, they dug a hole and buried Rill. Then one by one, they covered the grave with rocks. As much as Uri disliked Rill, he felt a deep sadness that stayed with him for a long time. He thought of when they came over to Dombara Land, and how Rill was so desperate to go home. Uri thought about the madness that would creep into Rill's eyes, and about all the schemes Rill had devised to hurt and destroy him. However, in the end Rill had destroyed himself.

Everyone was quiet on the walk back to the camp. Uri felt shaken by the violent events, and he knew everyone else was experiencing he same emotion. When they arrived at the camp Abosol started the fire again and made a pot of crost. They sat and quietly drank the hot soothing liquid.

"Now what?" asked Uri.

"We continue our mission." Coran said, staring into the fire. "Aleeta will be brought from the royal residence in the morning and handed over to me. Then we find Luwanna. Maybe Aleeta knows something about her location. We cannot expect to free her as easily as Aleeta. We were extremely fortunate Tri-Po wanted to get rid of her."

"You never told us why." Uri said.

"She was telling everyone about The Creator and His Son, our Savior." Coran smiled. "It caused quite a stir among the women caring for his wife, and his wife as well."

"Good for her." Jai laughed.

"Oden took off with our coins." Uri said. "We won't be able to pay for Luwanna's release, or buy anything in case we need to."

"True, we will have to make do with what we have.' Coran said then yawned. "Let's get some sleep before morning's light. Things will look brighter in the morning."

They agreed and lay down on their mats.

Chapter Twenty-Five
Together Again

Aleeta's heart pounded while the women she lived with for the past few weeks prepared her for a new owner. They perfumed the bath water, and combed her hair with sweet herbs. The dress was a smooth white fabric that draped over her frame softly, falling in folds to the floor. As Aleeta dressed, thoughts went to her betrothal day. She prayed soon to be back in Dombara Land with Coran, and continue what they had begun.

When she was ready to leave Aleeta gathered the women around Lai-Po. She sat on the edge of the bed. "My Lady, I will not be here when you give birth to your child. I wish I had been able to help you. I want all of you to remember the stories I told. However, they are not only stories but also true tales of the love our Creator and Savior have for us. Your rock-god is just that, a rock. It is only a creation of your tribe, and made with the hands of man. Creator of the Universe made every one of us. Call upon Him for understanding, and put your trust in Him alone." She hoped and prayed the seeds she planted would soon grow and flourish. In front of the entrance to the room appeared the men who guarded the house. "Tri-Po awaits you. It is time to leave." The head guard stepped forward. Polda began to cry again, and immediately they all were in tears.

"Goodbye." Aleeta gave each one a hug. Waving, she followed the escorts down the stairs and out into the sunlight.

Tri-Po entered the building at the center of the city dressed in ceremonial costume. He wanted to impress the travelers with a big showy ritual over this sale of Aleeta to this foreign visitor.

Guards escorted Aleeta over to the chieftain. She stopped and looked at the floor, careful not to raise her eyes. Coran stood at the edge of the steps, and watched her struggled to remain calm and nonresponsive. Crinkles began to show at the edges of his eyes.

Tri-Po cleared his throat and began to speak. "Our friends have come from the far north of this land. We welcome them into our homes and our people have enjoyed hearing of their different ways and the different culture. This man," he pointed to Coran. "has bought the slave girl called Aleeta. I will turn her over to him as he pays the tribute we agreed upon."

Behind Coran stood Abosol holding the two noogans. On the back of one lay a bolt of shimmering cloth.

Tri-Po reached for Aleeta's hand and led her down the steps to Coran, as Abosol led the animals up to him.

Coran accepted the small quivering hand of Aleeta. "Thank you for your hospitality." He bowed. "Now we must take our leave and continue the trek we started."

"Not so fast." Tri-Po said.

Aleeta's heart sprung into her throat and she felt herself freeze.

Coran opened his mouth to protest, but before he could speak, Tri-Po pointed over to the side of the building. There sat three large baskets laden with food.

132

"Our people wish to give you theses gifts to help you as you travel. After all, you have an extra mouth to feed."

Aleeta felt her legs wobble, and she tightened her grip on Coran's hand.

"My lord, how kind." Coran bowed again, deeply, and turned to the gathered crowd. "We accept your gifts and wish you well. Perhaps we will have the honor of visiting with you and your people again." He turned back to Abosol. They locked eyes and moved steadily toward their noogans to leave. Coran continued guiding Aleeta along without looking at her.

Abosol hoisted the baskets and placed them on his noogan behind the crowds.

Coran moved through the people gathered at the back of the central building, nodding and smiling. When they reached the animals, Coran lifted Aleeta on one and took the reins, guiding them along to the edge of the city. He put his finger to his lips to silence Aleeta until they had traveled out of range, and the city was behind them.

It seemed to take forever to reach the open meadow, beyond the cliffs. The sunshine glistened on the grasses. The sky above them was clear, and dazzled Aleeta's eyes. Then Coran stopped and gently lifted Aleeta down. She fell into his arms and their tears mixed as they kissed.

"How did you manage to buy me?" Aleeta asked.

"My darling, the leader Tri-Po wanted to get rid of you because you were reaching his wife and her attendants with the word of our Creator. He said you were creating a disturbance."

"Really, wonderful." Aleeta laughed.

133

"God is very good." Abosol sighed watching the couple. They began to retreat from the village and go into the woods back to their camp, where Uri and Jai waited.

xxx

"How magnificent is our Creator of All. How glorious is his Son who came into the Universe and died for us and took away all our sins." Coran stood in the middle of the camp. His arms lifted skyward. The sunshine fell between the leaves of the trees. Several insects flew about, and a hoperl peeked out from his home between the roots of a tree. Seeing the humans, he dropped back out of sight. Coran took Aleeta's hand, kissed her palm, and raised his arms again. "He has given our Aleeta back to us."

"Praise You, our Lord." Uri added. "May the seeds of Your truth Aleeta spread,grow among these people. Now Blessed Lord, we beseech you to help Luwanna. Set her free and send us to her."

"Amen." said Abosol.

Aleeta sat among them and began relating what she knew of Luwanna location. "She works in the fields. A friend of hers came to me and explained where she is living. There are large compounds where the outside workers stay. The compounds consist of eight women. An older woman lives in each compound to watch over them. I don't know which one Luwanna is in, or where she goes to work everyday."

"Is there someone you can contact who does know?" Uri asked.

"Her friend Tinra, but she won't be coming into town until the end of tomorrow. She visits her sister in a household at the end of the city."

"What time of day?" Coran holding her hand tightly.

"After supper, before sundown. She has to be back in her hut, in her bed shortly after sundown."

They ate an early dinner with some of the fruits and sweets the Umbinga's provided. Abosol quickly cooked several vegetables while they prayed and talked, serving it with fresh bread. In the back hills where the camp sat hidden, the group, which now included Aleeta, finished the meal in leisure, taking pleasure to enjoying this time. Coran cleared his throat and looked upwards at Aleeta. "Do you remember the man, Oden?"

"Why yes, he is half Dombara and half Mudan, right?" Aleeta answered.

"That is the one. He started the trip with us. Last night we caught him leaving camp without us. So we followed him." He finished relating the rest of the tale. Aleeta listened open mouthed her eyes wide with astonishment.

"Rill is really dead?" She whispered.

"Yes, we buried his body. However, Oden is loose, running around somewhere. We don't know if he will go back to his Mudan village or hide out here until we leave." Coran said.

"I believe the Creator will deal with him." Jai added, stuffing the last bite of bread in his already full mouth.

"Especially since he professed himself to be a believer." Uri replied as his picked up the dirty plates to stack them for Jai to clean.

"You don't think he will go after Luwanna, do you?" Aleeta replied. A shiver traveled through her body.

"I don't believe he will. That is not the way he thinks." Coran said.

135

"No, he is a coward and has probably hidden himself away." Uri spoke with disgust.

"Anyway, it is going to be a rough day tomorrow. Let's finish our chores, and get some rest." Coran suggested.

Chapter Twenty-Six
Finding Luwanna

Aleeta and Coran put their mats close together and snuggled down under their blankets. The fire flickered brightly and Coran put his arm around Aleeta.

"We haven't had any time to be together and talk." He said, almost in a whisper.

"I am just so happy to be with you." Aleeta responded.

"Were you treated well?"

"Yes, after we were free of Rill, and he turned us over to the Umbinga's, they cleaned us up, fed us, and gave us clean clothes. I could tell... they had been doing this a long time. There is a prescribed plan they follow. They questioned us about our abilities, and gave us a strength test." She giggled. "I failed." "So I was sent to do household chores, and ended up in the leader's house. Poor Luwanna was strong, so she was sent to work in the fields."

"What were your duties?" Coran said.

"My job was to massage oil on Lai-Po. She is very close to having her fifth child. Only one has lived." Aleeta frowned. "Do you know they do not allow their wives to do anything, I mean they do nothing at all. They eat only sweet and heavy foods. They have nothing healthy in their lives."

"Did you suggest exercise, fruits, and vegetables instead of sweet things?'

"Of course, but no one would listen to me. They scoffed at me. However, I did get them all to listen to the stories I told about the Creator of All. I believe I have planted good seeds."

Coran hugged her. "I am so happy to get you back." His eyes filled with tears.

When morning came Uri and Jai began to formulate a plan. They sat on a long, felled tree and drank their morning crost. They tossed ideas back and forth, finally deciding on a couple of feasible strategies.

"First we need to find the hut she lives." Uri said.

"Aleeta come over here." Jai called.

"Oh yes." Aleeta ran over to them and sat down.

"We must talk to her friend Tinra. Tell us how to find her sister's place."

"I have never been there." Aleeta began."However, she told me it is it is the first wooden building, just before the shops and businesses. The cliff homes are next to it. I think there is a narrow path between them."

Uri wrinkled his forehead. "I suppose we can hide there and watch for her as she comes down the street."

They got up and walked over to where Coran and Abosol worked cleaning up the camp.

"Have you thought of a plan?" Coran asked.

"Sort of…we have to talk to Tinra, and have her show us where Luwanna's hut is located." Uri began. "Later today we will go into the city and barter for a head-wrapping the same color as the guards, also a pair of those pants that they wear.

Since Abosol is the only one of us that looks like an Umbinga, he will dress up in them, and go to the hut where Luwanna is."

Jai cut in. "He will say the household of Tri-Po is asking for Luwanna. Then as Abosol heads back down the road with her, they will cut across the fields and run here. If all goes well we should be able to leave this place in the darkness of night."

"You will need to talk with their accent. Uri warned.

Abosol grinned. "No problem."

xxx

Uri and Jai arrived in the area of Tinra's sister home way before dusk. They flattened themselves against the rock wall in the narrow area between the homes and waited. It wasn't long before they saw the tall girl running down the road. Uri stepped out into the space between the houses and faced the road. As Tinra ran by, he called her name. She stopped, frozen and stared at Uri.

"I am Luwanna's friend. Please help me." Uri whispered and prayed she would come to him without anymore pleading.

"Who are you?" Tinra asked in a hushed voice.

"I am Uri."

Tinra looked up and down the street, and then proceeded cautiously toward him. The shadows of the houses concealed them well. When Tinra stood in front of him, he realized how tall she was and knew she came from the Mountain People.

"Do you want to help Luwanna?" he asked.

She looked from Uri to Jai. "Yes, she is my friend and fellow believer." She directed them under an area where the roof sloped low and hid them from the street. "How can I help?" She asked.

139

"We are tying to rescue her and bring her back home with us." Jai said. "However, we don't know where she is kept."

"How wonderful she has such friends." Tinra smiled. "I am here to see my sister. She is a slave in this household. When I leave, follow me. However, meander back and forth. Try not to act as if you are following me." With a nervous twitch, she glanced up and down the street. "I will leave the city on the main road and walk out to the fields. There isn't much foot traffic this time of the day. Watch and see which hut I enter. That is where Luwanna is."

"Good. If you can, let her know we will devise a plan to rescue her tomorrow, before dusk." Uri said.

The two patiently waited for Tinra to leave the house, with a quick pace, she walked back to the fields and into a hut that sat among many. Uri and Jai described to each other where this hut was located so they would not forget, and meandered back onto the path that lead to the hills and back to the camp.

When they arrived, the odor of dinner was tantalizing.

"What is that I smell, stew?" Jai cried.

"This is some of the bounty given to us by Tri-Po." Abosol said. "I mixed it up in a big pot with some of the noogan meat."

Uri laughed. "I think you are a better cook than Oden."

"I know I'm a better cook." he answered, and laughed gruffly.

Uri went over and sat next to Aleeta. "We found where Luwanna is staying."

"Oh, good." she replied.

Coran sat next to them and looked up at Jai and Abosol. "I have thought of a plan."

Everyone huddled around and listened.

Chapter Twenty-Seven
Rescue

Luwanna stepped through the doorway of her hut. She was exhausted and terribly dirty. The days seemed endless. The hope for a quick rescue was slipping away from her. She knew eventually that would happen, but maybe not as quickly as she had prayed it would.

Before she went to wash up, she fell on her bed and closed her eyes. Besides the ten-hour workdays, life had not been all that hard. There was plenty of food, not exciting, but filling. There was some freedom. The girls could walk and talk among themselves after work, and before bedtime. Volma was strict, but kind and the Umbinga people were diligent at caring for everyone's health. There were the male guards everywhere, coming, and going. They patrolled the fields daily. It seemed to Luwanna that most of the girls had completely resigned themselves to their condition. Luwanna had not heard any talk of plans of escaping from anyone. Slavery was a way of life here, expected and reaffirmed.

Her friend Tinra had tried to talk to her about something all day, however there was never a chance to be alone. After dinner she would go outside and motion to Tinra to follow. It must be important, maybe a message from Aleeta.

Luwanna looked at her hands. They were rough and dirty. Many sores, new and old ones in various stages of healing, covered the front and backs of her hands. Her bad arm hurt day and night. She longed for the comfort of her home, bed, and most of all Uri. She fought the tears; they didn't help, so she stood up to walk to the back of the hut where the washbasin sat. It was at that moment she noticed a commotion and voices at the door of the hut.

"Who are you?" Volma asked. "I haven't seen you before."

"I am a new guard, from Tri-Po's Royal Residence." the inflection in the voice brought in memories of her Pinola home. As Luwanna whirled around, she didn't recognize Abosol at the entrance to the hut. Dressed in a guard uniform, he stood erect, holding the sword in his left hand. The yellow headdress of a guard was wrapped tightly on his head with the proper tassels hanging from the top. His pants were a little tight for him, but they also were the proper style and color. However, something was out of place.

Luwanna stood frozen as this strange guard addressed Volma again. "I have been sent by the household to bring the slave, Luwanna to Tri-Po." He glared at Volma, and added. "Immediately."

"She hasn't washed from being in the fields yet." Volma answered.

"She can wash at the palace."

Volma sighed and motioned for Luwanna to come forward. "Go with this man." she ordered.

Luwanna lowered her eyes and walked out the door in front of Abosol. She intuitively knew something was happening, and she peeked up at this large man that looked and spoke like an Umbinga.

"Be quiet." Abosol ordered her. "When we get around the bend, start running for the hills."

Now she realized this was someone attempting to rescue her.

They had walked about 100 feet from the hut, when another guard came up running.

Luwanna stiffened, looking behind her to see if anyone could see them, but they had gone beyond that bend in the road, and were out of sight of the huts.

She saw Abosol braced himself for a confrontation.

"Halt!" The guard yelled. "Who are you and where are you going with this slave?"

"I have instructions to take her to the residence of Tri-Po. They have sent for her."

"You are not familiar to me. I do not believe you. You are taking her away." The guard raised his sword, but before he could get it into a fighting position. Abosol lowered his head and ran full force at the guard's stomach. The man fell to the ground and Abosol pounding his fist into the guards face. Suddenly another ran into the fracas. He bent over Abosol in an effort to pull him off the unconscious guard. Luwanna acted quickly, and doubling her fists together, she rammed them into the back of his neck. He moaned and fell off the men onto the ground. Abosol pick up the guard's head, and slammed it into the ground for good measure, then grabbed Luwanna's hand. They ran like the wind, over the fields and up into the hills.

They ran until Luwanna couldn't breath anymore. Her lungs burned and she had a pain in her right side.

"Don't stop." Abosol urged her. "We are almost there."

"I'll try." She gasped. The trees and bushes were all around them now and the fields far behind. Luwanna fell, and then got up. She was wobbly, but took a deep breath and began to run again.

"That'a girl." Abosol said breathlessly.

Finally, they stopped running. Luwanna fell over a large rock and gasped for breath.

"I have never run so far or so fast in my whole life." Her words staggered out in a moan. She looked up at Abosol, who bent over struggling for air. "Why are you here?"

"Coran got me to help. I track." He managed to say.

"Oh…well, thank you." Luwanna rolled off the rock and sat on the ground. "Have you found Aleeta?"

"Yes, she is with us at camp, waiting for you. Everyone is waiting for you."

"That was a very brave thing you did. Crazy, but brave." Luwanna stood up, and walk over to Abosol. She reached down and kissed his cheek. Blushing, he stood straight.

"You saved my life." Luwanna said.

"The only reason I was chosen is because I'm ugly, like the Umbingas."

"Nonsense." Luwanna laughed. "You are beautiful, big and strong. Also your hair is dark."

He unwrapped the turban that covered the top of his head and threw it on the ground. "Are you ready to continue?" he asked.

"Yes."

They walked down the twisted trail and soon Luwanna heart leapt in her chest when she saw Uri in front of her. She began to sob, walked the next few paces, and collapsed into his arms..

xxx

The group left the hills surrounding the city of the Umbinga's almost immediately after Luwanna and Abosol joined them. It was certain the tribe would send guards into the hills, looking for any trace of them. It was only a matter of time before they put the foreign travelers together with Luwanna's disappearance. In the dark of night, the six figures, with the animals, crept in silence through the hills and out onto the meadow, by the rivers and lakes. Here they could see a search party coming in the distance.

"We will bed down here. The group of trees will give us some shelter. I will stay on watch while you all sleep for a few hours." Coran volunteered.

"That's a good idea. The girls are exhausted and we guys aren't doing much better either." Jai said.

They rolled out their mats and within minutes the sound of snoring made Coran smile.

Uri woke to the brightest morning he had seen in a long time. He looked over to Luwanna, next to him, sleeping peacefully. A light blanket covered her slender frame. Once again, the peaceful beauty of this area enthralled Uri. He sat up and let his eyes soak up the green colors of the grasses, trees, and clear blue water of the lakes and streams.

The desire to return rose up in him, as before. He thought, *"How could a place, so peaceful and beautiful become dangerous? It doesn't seem right."* As he looked down Luwanna's open eyes were staring at him.

"Oh, you are awake now," he said.

"Yes, I watched your face as you looked over the landscape. You have fallen in love with this place, haven't you?" Luwanna sat up. "It is stunning."

"I would like to come back here some day." Uri stated, with softness in his voice.

Luwanna touched his arm and smiled. "We will come back someday. There are many situations that need to be changed here."

"I would like that, if it is the Lord's will." He answered.

They looked into each other's eyes for a long moment.

Everyone began to move about the camp. A few hours sleep would have to do, for surely the Umbingas would be close behind.

Then Abosol let out a loud yawn and hollered. "Everybody… grab something to eat and pack up. Let's go."

Jai, standing near the campfire yelled and pointed to the distant trees. "Look, someone is coming this way. She is running."

Luwanna shaded her eyes against the sun. "It looks like Tinra."

They all watched as the girl stumbled into camp, gasping for breath. "They are coming," she said.

"Come sit down." Jai led her to a rock. "Get your breath and then tell us."

Luwanna ran to Tinra's side, and grabbed her hand. "Are the guards following us?"

Tinra nodded. "As soon as I heard they were gathering up the guards to follow after you, I began running."

"Do they have weapons?" Uri asked.

"Spears." Tinra took a deep breath. "Someone told Tri-Po about Luwanna, and he concluded he was tricked by the

147

travelers that bought Aleeta. He became furious. Then he ordered the guards to follow and bring both the girls back."

"You took a big risk by coming here and warning us." Coran said.

"Yes, by now they know I am not in my hut, and haven't gone to work." Tinra nodded.

"What are you going to do?" Luwanna asked. "They will punish you, especially if they find out you came to warn us."

"I left from my sister's place. When I return I will stay there and pretend I got sick. She will cover for me."

Jai bent over her. "Why don't you come with us?"

"I can't leave my sister." she hung her head. "Otherwise, I would."

Coran helped her up. "Then you must go back quickly, before they arrive. You will have to take another route otherwise you will run into them coming here."

"I have that all planned." Tinra answered.

"Are you sure you won't come with us. You can come and live in my father's home. We have plenty of room." Jai pleaded.

"I'm sorry. I must stay."

Coran gave her some water in a pouch. "Here, take this with you."

"Thank you. You are all very kind. I must go now."

Luwanna watched sadly as her friend crossed the meadow, and disappeared into the forest..

"Hurry, everyone." Urged Abosol. "We need to get packed up and leave. In the hills we can find a place to defend ourselves, should it come to that."

They left, hurrying along the trail to the hills. Uri, Coran and Abosol pulled their noogans, loaded with supplies behind them. The sun was starting down from the zenith by the time the group reached the top of the hills. Here they could look back over the meadow from which they had come.

It was very cold there. Spots of white clung to the ground in the shadows, here and there. The girls shivered as Abosol broke out the coats from a pack. He gave Aleeta and Luwanna each one.

Jai stood guard, looking from the peak into the valley below as the others rested for a few moments.

"I need to tell you the stories that Tinra related to me about the Umbingas." Luwanna spoke with haste. "I had long talks with Tinra. She was trained in writing, and was gifted in this art. The men who keep the customs and history of the Umbingas used her to write down on paper, their legends. They went as far back as to when they lived in a different land."

"Go on." Uri urged, edging closer to her.

"They lived in a place far to the north where a large river met the sea. They grew crops, had some animals for food and milk, and the weather was mild and wet. They worshiped their Rock God and he blessed them. Life was good. They flourished for many years. Then things began to change. The weather grew warmer and dry. The river level dropped. Crops began to fail and the animals grew weak. For several years, they struggled. The women started to grow weak from continued hunger and the babies died.

"That was when the men changed their attitude toward the women and began to pamper them. They gave all the food they had to the women and children. It got very bad, so they built large boats from the trees around them, and left their homes to row across the sea. They didn't know where they were going or what they would find, but if they stayed all would die."

"Then what happened?" Uri asked.

"They sailed to the land where they live now. Arriving, they followed a river upstream and came across the beautiful valley, where they settled. That was many, many years ago." she paused. "That is the entire story."

Uri knew the Umbingas were descendents of the people that lived in Pinola Land, near the sea. The mystery was solved and the story now complete. Some of them must have stayed and moved into where the Pinola Tribe now live. That is why both tribes share the same features.

In the distance, Jai saw the row of guards emerge from the forest into the meadow. "They are coming!" he warned.

They will be here in a short while." Cautioned Coran. "They don't have any animals or supplies to slow them down."

"The girls need to keep on moving. However, when we reach the place by the tree and the moving rocks, the rest of us can stand our ground." Coran said. He looked over at Jai.

"Take the girls and one noogan loaded with supplies. Leave immediately, travel quickly, and don't look back."

Coran and Uri watched as the girls waved while following Jai down and path and out of sight.

Chapter Twenty Eight
The Moving Rocks

When Coran, Uri, and Abosol looked down into the valley late in the afternoon, the guards were climbing up the path between the cliffs.

Moving on to the place where the rocks surrounded the lone tree, the three sat on the ground to rest and wait.

"Coran and I are the ones Tri-Po dealt with." Abosol said. "Uri can pretend he is the tender of our animals. This way they will see we don't have Aleeta or Luwanna."

"They will ask where Aleeta is." Uri said.

"She escaped." Abosol offered.

"Do you think Oden went to Tri-Po?" Uri asked.

"I think Oden is trying to get us killed." Abosol said.

"Probably so." Coran agreed. "He is still attempting to cover his misdeeds. However, here we are... simple travelers. The Umbingas cannot prove otherwise."

"Oden will tell them we came here to take the girls back." Uri said.

"We have no girls, so it is his word against ours. In addition, he has something to hide, Rill's death." Coran pointed out.

Uri sat and played with the small pebbles, moving them around and noticed, while most attracted each other, there were a few that moved away from each other. He pondered that, and wondered what made some do that. His Yoka teacher recently taught him about a strange force that existed in the Universe. This force kept the heavenly bodies moving around each other. This must be the same type of force on a smaller scale, of course. However, why some attract, and some repel?

They didn't have to wait long for the troops to overtake them. As they marched into the area where the men sat, Uri moved closer to the larger rocks.

Oden ran in front of Tri-Po's men. "Here they are. They are the ones." He yelled.

The head of the guards walked slowly over to them and looked down. "Where are the slaves girls, Aleeta and Luwanna?"

"Look around," Coran answered. "Do you see anyone else here except for us?"

"They are hiding them, I tell you." Oden was goading the man on.

"Look for yourselves. Only the three of us are here." Coran's hand swept the area.

"Where is the slave you received from Tri-Po, where is the slave Aleeta?" the head guard asked.

"She escaped in the middle of the night." Abosol lied. He had no problem telling a straight- faced lie, whereas he knew Coran could not. Abosol continued, "There is no one else here."

Uri stood up. "Did your friend Oden tell you he killed the Dombara called Rill?"

The head of the guard looked puzzled.

"He is a liar and a murderer." Uri pointed to Oden and accused him outright.

Oden emitted a nervous laugh. "Why would I kill Rill?"

"Rill knew something about him that would cause the Dombaras to arrest him." Uri continued. "He disposed of the evidence, which was Rill."

Oden turned to the guards in an effort to distract them. "Look, I have something magical. It is from the rock-god, given especially to me. Watch!"

Pulling something from his pocket, he moved toward the tree with the rocks surrounding it. He grinned at the head of the guards and showed him a large stone. Uri knew immediately it was one Oden picked up, and hid in his pocket when they first came through this place.

"Magic from the rock god." Oden moved the large stone over the pile of rocks. Some leapt up and attached themselves to his stone, larger ones moved around the ground. The guards gasped, and moved back.

"It is magic from the rock-god." Cried the head guard.

"No, no!" cried Uri. "This is not Oden's magic from the rock god. I can make the rocks move also."

He ran and grabbed a larger stone than Oden's and ran around the tree. Everything on the ground wiggled and moved all at once, following Uri. "They move at my command." Uri said and found the ones that repelled. "See some move away and I command some to follow." He walked backwards, held the stone in front of him, making the rocks move, wiggle, and jump up. He caused some to attach to the large stone.

"Ay..." cried one of the guards. "They both have magic! We must leave this evil place."

The head guard, visibly shaken, motioned for retreat. The terrified men fled in the direction of the path they came from. Oden glared menacingly at Uri then turned and ran, close behind the guards while crying, "Wait... wait." They all quickly disappeared.

Uri couldn't help himself. He doubled over with laughter. Coran and Abosol, joined in.

Still chuckling, they moved over to the edge of the peak to watch. Soon, Coran pointed at the men moving through the meadow in disarray. Oden was not with them.

"I wonder where Oden went." Uri asked. "Do you think he will come back after us?"

"No, he doesn't have the stomach for a fight." Coran answered with sadness in his voice. "He is a man without a tribe. He will be a wanderer from now on. He can no longer go to the Mudan, Dombara, or Bast tribes."

"He might be able to mingle with the Umbinga's." Uri said.

"I doubt the Umbinga's would trust him anymore." Abosol commented.

"There is always the shadowy existence in every tribe. The unsavory night people that move, and live with the shadows." Uri spoke with an edge to his voice.

"He might fit in there." Coran pondered that thought.

Uri began to shiver for a cold wind began to blow through the area. The mild spell was coming to an end. Now, in the distance beyond the mountaintops, dark clouds gathered.

154

Soon blowing wind, laced with white frozen raindrops would obscure the entire mountainside.

Uri took the rope tied to Igi, his noogan, and led him down the path. Coran and Abosol followed close behind, leaving the ugliness, and beauty of the land where the Umbingas lived.

Chapter Twenty Nine
Celebrating Home

An afternoon breeze playfully wafted across the play field. It touched the tips of leaves and caressed the colored streamers set up at the edges of the area decorated for the wedding. The sun beamed in a cloudless sky, and the Dombaras mingled among themselves in a holiday mood. Finally, the long awaited joining of Aleeta and Coran was moments away.

The haunting tones of a flute began in the background and everyone turned to watch the bride emerge from the canvas tent set up just for her, and her entourage.

Uri and Jai stood next to the tent, and watched Cherka, Jai's sister step out first. She held a box that carried the ring Coran would place on Aleeta's left thumb and the beaded bracelet for Coran. That bracelet marked the wearer married, therefore unavailable to maidens in the village. The child Cherka, was tall for her seven years, and took her duties very seriously.

Luwanna emerged next. Uri felt his heart swell at the sight of her. She wore a pale blue dress with a golden sash tied at her small waist and blue ribbons in her hair, flowing down her back. Her golden tresses gleamed in the sunlight. Then Aleeta stepped out. Her white dress was twice as beautiful as her betrothal gown. Her Marmie, Prisea had sewn tiny, shining beads on the bodice and around the hem. At her waist was a blue sash. It was tied at the side, and fell in folds down to the hem of the dress. Her gleaming auburn hair, pulled to the back and braided, shone with thin slivers of golden ribbons. Across her face, at the nose and mouth, hung a fine veil of golden threads. Uri gasped at how beautiful she looked. From her eyes, the thin, frail girl showed strength and determination. How they sparkled as she looked from face to face.

The trio walked up to the front of the crowd and stood next to the priest, Elari.

The crowd parted as Coran, flanked by Jai's father, Ando, and Coran's father Kinter marched down the path. Coran wore the blue robe over the linen of a priest. He had a golden crown on his head and fine golden chains hanging from the robe. His eyes met Uri's and crinkled at the edges.

"What a glorious day." Uri thought. Everyone had feared this day would never come to be. However, the God of the Universe was in control, and He had designed their lives.

Uri reflected back to the long and strenuous trip from the Land of the Umbingas. It took several days for them to recover. Even Abosol was laid up with his feet bloodied and raw. The girls had gone to recuperate at Jai's home where specials attendants could care for them.

As soon as Coran felt strong enough, he began to plan for this wedding day. Coran and Aleeta hadn't wanted to wait any longer. Now, Uri began to find himself thinking about his own wedding day, and how he would feel, walking toward Luwanna, as she stood beside the priest. Would it be Coran? What would she be wearing? Uri shook his head. *"Back to the present,"* he sternly told himself.

The reading of the vows began. Then quickly as it started, they were wed, and the priest sprinkled water over them, declaring they were as one. The crowd cheered, and the newlyweds threw colored beads into the crowd.

"The God of the Universe is pleased," Elari cried loudly. "Rejoice, eat, drink, and celebrate this grand day."

Everyone began to laugh, cry, and hug the happy couple. Finally, they all sat down to eat the food prepared by loving hands. Celebrating lasted late into the night. Even Uri and his family stayed later than they had planned.

Eventually, Elajon carried a snoring Bibbi in his arms, while Uri lugged Sarella, sleeping with her head over his shoulder, home and into bed.

xxx

Summer days began to shorten, and nights grew cooler. The days of danger and adventure melted into days of leisure. Jai, Luwanna, Bibbi, and Uri spent the last couple of weeks boating, laying around at the park, or playing the game of Cussel on the floor of Prisea's house.

It was evening, on a crisp, early fall day when they left Prisea's hut on the water's edge. After walking Luwanna to her parents home, Bibbi left to gather with his friends for a while at the park as Jai and Uri arrived at the steps of the grand house of Ando, Jai's father. They sat down on the first step, watching the sun sink low over the town.

"What now?" Uri asked his friend. "Do you have plans for the future?"

"I have decided to register for the advanced school. I want to be my father's aid, and learn about working in the ruling body of our tribe."

"Isn't that what your father wanted Goth to do?" Uri asked.

"Goth didn't have any interest in that. He loves animals so that is why he and Lyshon acquired the farm, and are raising kavaks and noogans. They are doing very well, I might add."

"We need to do what we are led to do." Uri said.

"What about you?" Jai asked Uri.

"I'm going to school as you. Also... I have decided to go into the priesthood."

"Somehow I am not surprised." Jai smiled.

"I have talked to Coran, and I will probably start with the indoctrination next month. It will be two afternoons a week"

"Is he going to sponsor you?" Jai asked.

"Yes. There is something else." Uri took a deep breath.

"Go on." urged Jai.

"I want to marry Luwanna."

Jai grinned and then began laughing. "Ah... How does she feel about that?"

"I don't know." Uri felt his heart tremble. "She hasn't given me any indication she cares the same way I do." He paused. "It's not funny Jai."

"I know. It's...it's, well... I should have guessed. However, don't jump into anything. Go slow with her. We are all still very young." Jai advised. "Also, you have a lot of schooling to go through."

Uri frowned, "I didn't say I wanted to marry her tomorrow." He stood up, irritated with Jai's reaction. "I only want to talk to her about it. We need to plan our future."

"I will pray for you and your future with Luwanna. You two would make a great team."

"Thanks." Uri turned to go. "Goodnight, I will see you tomorrow."

"Goodnight Uri, and the Lord bless you both."

Chapter Thirty
The Future

Early afternoon the next day, Jai and Uri walked along the path that led to the middle of the town. They had gone to the Advanced School of Learning to look the rooms over and so Jai could flirt with the lovely girl who sat behind the table in the main building. Uri's questions for her were mainly about the days and times of the math and history classes. Jai's questions were only about her. The next stop for Uri would be the headquarters for the priesthood. He needed to sign up for the beginning studies.

The air had grown cooler and damp. Uri hated this type of weather when he first arrived in Dombara Land. Now it was comfortable and indicated happy, exciting times. The summer days had moved into fall, and the two friends talked about how they felt as many things ended. A door was closing on part of their lives. From leaving Pinola Land, to all the adventures he experienced, he now looked forward to a new and exciting future that lay ahead.

Uri left Jai at the front of the grand home he shared with his sister Cherka, Frash his younger brother, and his parents. Uri then started down the path to the building that housed the leaders of their faith. He would be moving into this building after the beginning studies were finished and he graduated to religious classes. At midway, Uri passed a large tree. It reminded him of the Tobanyant tree that grew in front of Beka and Suwat's home, in Pinola Land. Uri paused, then sat in its shade and rested against the trunk. He closed his eyes, and gave himself permission to relax and enjoy the soft breeze. It seemed a lifetime had passed since he sat on the Pinola sand dunes, enjoying the breeze filter over the desert. Then, Uri, at the age of fourteen years, was determined to be a hunter. He fancied himself the greatest hunter of the desert worm, the wona, in the entire Pinola kingdom. He was satisfied with his life when the Dombaras came and kidnapped all of the children in his village. The trauma of the separation from his Pinola family, and the shocking revelation that they all were born Dombaras rocked his world to the very foundation. He was determined to go home, back to the Pinola Land, and Rill became part of the plan to escape. However, Uri almost died after being lost at sea, and he thought Rill had actually drowned.

Through a quirk of fate, the man who had injured his sister, Beka and captured him was also his cousin, Coran. Because of Coran's visions, he was the one who rescued Uri off the sand bar, and from that time on, one of Uri's closest companions. Since that time, he found himself in the middle of mysteries: poisonings, dealing with the Bast Tribe, and Rill's return armed with evil, vengeful plots. Through these adventures, Uri experienced a compelling fervor to acquire the ability to reveal the knowledge of The Creator's redeeming grace, and bring a better way of life to all tribes in this world. Uri's experience with the Umbinga Tribe, and their dysfunctional culture had only intensified this desire.

A bird rested in the tree above him, and began a noisy scolding, so Uri rose and continued his trek. The play field came into view and he detoured over to get a drink from the fountain. In his mind, he could hear the echoes of Bibbi playing cho ball with his friends. The memories of the clandestine meetings with Rill, as they planned their escape, and times he strolled with Luwanna through and around the paths, drifted up

162

to fill his mind in no apparent pattern. He shuddered at the image of the getiru that attacked Luwanna, and he smiled to himself at the thought of how bravely she risked her life in order to rescued him from the Bast people.

"Wow," Uri thought, *"I'm in a pensive mood."*

He got his drink and a figure came into view as he looked over to the path he had crossed. He couldn't mistake the golden curls, the beautiful dark, golden eyes, and the smile he loved so much.

"Hi, Uri. Where are you going?" Luwanna spoke.

"I am heading over to the priest center," he replied.

"What are you going to do over there?"

"Sign up." Uri grinned.

"Let's sit down and talk this over." Luwanna said, looking very wise. "I want to know what is going on."

They found a bench and he turned to face her. Now was a good time to talk to her about the future and his intentions.

"I have decided what I want to do." He began. "I want to study to be a priest."

"Why?" Was the only thing Luwanna asked.

"I have always felt that Coran does so much good. I want to do good, also."

"So, you want to be a priest because Coran is one." Luwanna had a way of cutting through to the heart of things.

"No, you misunderstand. I want to bring the news of the Savior and our Creator to people who are in bondage to superstition and false beliefs." Uri said thoughtfully. "I want to learn everything I can about the character of The Creator, and try to be like Him."

163

"That's better. Nevertheless, you are different from Coran, and The Creator has other plans for your life."

"I know that!" Uri frowned. "I guess you don't understand what is in my heart."

Luwanna slid closer to him. She looked intensely into his eyes. "What is in your heart?"

Uri felt his pulse quicken. Only she could drive him from one emotion to another so rapidly. "I have many things in my heart. You are one of them."

Luwanna lowered her eyes. "You are in my heart too."

"You see, we are still very young." Uri said, "I'm almost eighteen and you are just sixteen. After four years of schooling and training, we will be grown, and able to make important decisions about our lives."

"We can make important decisions now," Luwanna said softly. "I always have known what I wanted." She put her hand over his.

The shock that traveled through his body caused Uri to jump. She cut to the heart of his desire.

"Don't toy with me, say what you mean." Uri picked up her hand in his. "I want to marry you…someday. It can't be now, so we have to be cautious. We have been friends since you were very little. That should be how things remain."

"Oh Uri, you are so practical. I want to spend the rest of my life with you and share your passion for helping others. I know we have to wait, and we will continue to be friends forever. Now that we know how we feel, there is more than friendship. There is love between us. That feeling cannot be denied. We can't pretend it doesn't exist."

Uri was quiet for a long time. "I don't know how to act," he finally admitted.

Luwanna smiled and touched his face.

"We go on the way we always have. Now we share a secret. I care about you and you care about me. We can be together as usual, however now there will be more joy in it."

"People will see our joy," he whispered.

"Good, there is no need to hide. Eventually everyone will share in that joy." Luwanna stood. "Now you go to see Coran and I will go home and help with dinner. When you are done, come to my house and join us. That is not anything new, right?"

Uri nodded. He turned Luwanna's hand palm up. He gently kissed it. "See you later." He smiled and watched as she walked away.

His future was in both directions. Down the path to Luwanna's home and up the path to the priesthood.

Uri was very happy.

Epilogue

The years of Uri's schooling went by swiftly. He and Luwanna married four years from the date he entered the learning center. Immediately they went to live in Umbinga land, near the lakes and meadow Uri had fallen in love with years before.

Their influence on the Umbinga Tribe was nothing less than a miracle. Uri convinced the elders of the tribe to allow their women independence, and Luwanna began a program for the women to understand what it was to be healthy. It wasn't long before the slaves became paid servants and developed lives of their own.

Turning from their beliefs in the rock-god took longer. Bit by bit individuals came to join the prayer and learning groups. Uri held his youngest child a girl named Kerka, as he related stories of the Savior's life, death, and resurrection while Luwanna taught her two boys practical studies with some of the Umbinga children. Their pleasure and satisfaction grew with each passing year.

They both lived long, useful lives. Raised three children, saw eleven grandchildren come into the world and four great-grandchildren. They brought the knowledge of The Creator of All, and His Savior to the Umbinga Tribe and watched while the people increased in love and devotion to each other.

Because of Uri's influence, the Pinola Tribe and the Umbinga Tribe became believers. In that, Uri and Luwanna fulfilled the work God gave them to do.

Made in the USA
San Bernardino, CA
18 January 2014